The Mount of the Holy Cross

Apparently Dr. Leach had heard something, for he cocked his head to one side, and then Frank heard it too: a subdued moaning in the far distance, sounding like the bleak wailing of a prairie wind, or a beast in pain trapped in the bowels of the earth. It might have been his imagination (he wasn't sure), but Frank also thought he felt a tremor pass through the soles of his feet, a low frequency vibration which seemed to jar the fillings in his teeth.

He looked questioningly at the others, who had frozen in attitudes of listening, and then his attention was caught and held by the expression on Dr. Leach's face. He had seen people under hypnosis and the scientist reminded him of someone in a state of trance, lost to this world and inhabiting a region beyond the normal senses, where the private inner visions of the mind constitute the single ultimate reality...

THIS
SENTIENT
EARTH

Trevor Hoyle

ZEBRA BOOKS

KENSINGTON PUBLISHING CORP.

ZEBRA BOOKS
are published by
KENSINGTON PUBLISHING CORP.
21 East 40th Street
New York, N.Y. 10016

First Printing: April, 1979

Printed in the United States of America

Author's Apologia

It is the science fiction writer's privilege (and pleasure) to tamper with the geography of this planet, though in this instance I feel an apology is due to those kind people who live along the Roaring Fork Valley in Colorado, USA. Not only have I moved several towns in the vicinity, like chess pieces, to suit my narrative, but I've also cast some of the citizens of Gypsum as characters—all of whom, needless to say, are fictitious (the characters, not the citizens).

In my defense I can only plead that finding a mountain called the Mount of the Holy Cross exactly where I wanted it to be was far too good an opportunity to miss. So if the people of Gypsum must blame somebody or something, please blame the mountain. It's big enough to look after itself.

Part One

THE MOUNTAIN

CHAPTER ONE

The travel-streaked red Oldsmobile Toronado turned onto Interstate 70 north of Grand Junction and headed east along the rift known as Roaring Fork Valley: it was then that Frank Kersh got his first glimpse of the mountain. It rose up directly in front of him, a vast cruel wall of granite hewn by wind, water and ice, towering over the slender winding ribbon of road, dominating the valley and casting its long ragged shadow across the descending banks of green and golden aspens.

This part of Colorado was new to him, although two years before he had visited the Martin Marietta Space Center near Denver on an assignment for *Science Now.* The subject had been the joint USA-USSR space shuttle which NASA was keen to develop, but since then precious little had been heard of it, and, Frank suspected, even less achieved. It was one more example of scientific cooperation foiled by political tomfoolery. Frank Kersh didn't care for politicians, having seen them slash research budgets for no good reason save that of appeasing an indifferent and ill-informed electorate.

6

Steering carefully with one hand he checked his map and found what he was looking for: the Mount of the Holy Cross, a 14,000-foot high peak overlooking the Eagle River and the small townships dotting its banks—De Beque, Rifle, Silt, New Castle, Dotsero, Eagle—and the place he was heading for, Gypsum, the nearest town to the Rocky Mountain Neutrino Astrophysical Research Station. Known in scientific circles as "Deep Hole," the Project had taken over an old disused gold mine and installed equipment in what was reputedly the deepest mining shaft in the United States. The strange thing, as Frank now reflected, was that a two-year 1½ million-dollar research program had produced hardly anything in the way of new scientific data; a couple of routine progress reports from the Project leader, Professor Edmund Friedmann, had appeared in the scientific press but these had been concerned with method and application rather than factual information which added significantly to high energy solar particle research.

In fairness it had to be said that results weren't rated by the speed with which they were obtained —it wasn't a case of the faster the better—yet even so something more positive might have been reasonably expected from a team of experienced scientists and research workers using the world's most advanced neutrino detection equipment. Hence the reason for the current assignment, which Perry Tolchard, Frank's editor, had as an afterthought added to the list. "It might make a short filler for the 'Feedback' page. Don't spend more than a day there, Frank, it isn't worth it."

"Should I check out the Denver Space Center while I'm in the vicinity?"

"If you have time. Give them a call and find out if anything's happening that NASA have recently declassified."

So he had planned his schedule accordingly: arriving in Gypsum during the late afternoon, the following day to be spent out at the Deep Hole Project, and then moving on to the Martin Marietta Space Center. There was no real hurry to get back to Chicago, and after the long drive from the West Coast he felt he deserved a period of relative relaxation.

To his right the Eagle River drifted calmly between low sandy banks, occasionally speeding up and turning to white rough water as it negotiated a sharp bend or a rocky outcrop. The highest state in the nation, Colorado was a land which straddled the Rockies, the result of half a billion years of cataclysmic forces which had repeatedly ripped the bedrock apart and flung up massive mountain ranges, which were then eroded by violent storms and flooding by encroaching seas. Volcanic activity caused more disruption, the seething lava bringing up precious minerals from the Earth's core until 80 million years ago the vast ragged-toothed panorama of soaring peaks and deep sharp ravines cooled and crystallized, trapping veins of gold, silver, zinc, lead, molybdenum and uranium. A hundred years ago the area had been a prospectors' paradise, the lure of gold bringing men from every corner of the country with the promise of striking it rich. Some of the townships had carried the legend into the

20th century, their names a testament to those early pioneering days of exploration and discovery: Leadville, Basalt, Troublesome, Carbondale, Radium, and the more enigmatically-named Climax, Paradox and Breckenridge.

It was still wild terrain, an area of dense forests and lost trails leading to forgotten workings and bleak inhospitable heights which spent many of their days shrouded in swirling mist. And even now in early September, Frank could see that some of the taller peaks were capped with a fine powdering of snow.

Nearer now, the Mount of the Holy Cross seemed to lean right over him. He thought: It's so intimidating it could almost be alive. The people living round here must always be conscious of its looming presence, a severe granite face watching all that they do, reading their minds, ruling their lives.

The sign ahead said *Dotsero*, the last town before Gypsum. They were all the same, these places out here in the back of beyond. A main street with stores, a couple of bars, a post office, a small wooden-fronted hotel with a porch. He wondered idly what the people found to do when the winter snows blocked the passes and cut them off from the rest of civilization. They had TV and perhaps a Saturday night dance, but for Frank, a city boy born and bred, he couldn't imagine how they lasted through the long winter months. And the scientists on the Deep Hole Project were even more isolated, living in their small self-contained community with not much to occupy their minds beyond the highly-specialized field of solar neutrino research.

The last lingering rays of the sun sent slanting

shadows across the road in front of him. It was a smooth undulating black snake following the line of the river to his right, and further beyond the gradual slopes of the aspens on the foothills to the deceptively gentle shoulders of the mountain itself. For the life of him he couldn't dismiss the mountain from his thoughts: it seemed to be blocking out the sky, a monstrous presence dominating everything.

He had read somewhere—a legend of an ancient superstitious people—that mountains embodied the spirits of dead ancestors. It had meant very little to him when he had read it, but now the awful reality of such a belief made itself felt. You only had to approach a mountain to feel the essence of something real and vital and alive . . . in this case a force that seemed almost malignant in its brooding proximity.

Frank Kersh shivered and gripped the wheel tighter. This was silly. He wasn't at all superstitious, he was a science writer with a degree in biochemistry, a rational mind and a routine assignment to fulfill. Tonight he would sleep in the shadow of the mountain and tomorrow he would visit the Project; the day after he would be on his way.

A single shaft of sunlight illuminated the sign at the roadside and the dust-covered Oldsmobile Toronado rolled into the town of Gypsum.

CHAPTER TWO

The Cascade Hotel was a three-story red brick building on the main square, directly opposite the Courthouse. At this hour the town was quite busy as the store-keepers locked up for the night and the clerks from the offices and banks made their way home along the neat sidewalks. Frank was struck by the primness of the town; he had expected it to have a raw, almost rugged quality, a nostalgic throwback to the old mining days, but instead the place had acquired an air of faded gentility as if pretending that its rough romantic past had never existed. It reminded him of a person with a closed mind.

He took his leather grip from the rear seat of the car and entered the hotel. He had plans for a shower, a couple of stiff drinks, dinner, and an early night. He really was weary. It wasn't just the long drive, he told himself. The truth was he was out of shape: at thirty-three he was paying the penalty for the sedentary life-style of a writer, swapping an office chair for the driving seat and using elevators in-between. And the pity of it was that not so long ago—eighteen months, two years—he had been pretty active, out most weekends

11

with the Cicero Explorers, camping up at Green Bay in northern Wisconsin with a full program of trekking, pot-holing and dry-suit aqualung diving off Beaver Island. But about that time he had taken on the job of associate editor with *Science Now* which meant more commitment, longer hours, and weekends taken up with planning conferences and last-minute rewrites for the next edition. Perry had warned him about the workload and said in the same breath (which was full of pipe smoke) that he musn't let recreation get in the way of his career. The journal was the fastest-growing science monthly in North America and with an increasing circulation overseas; in other words, Frank thought wryly, stick with us, baby, and we'll make you a star.

There was a real live cowboy in the lobby, with Stetson and spurs, who glanced up as Frank went past the overstuffed armchairs and the brass cuspidor toward the desk. They were either saving power or had forgotten to turn the lights on and the place was in semi-darkness, the gathering twilight making areas of dense shadow and filling the interior with a soft brown dusk.

The cowboy was stretched out on a couch by the window, his hat tipped forward, and although his eyes couldn't be seen Frank knew he was being observed each step of the way.

He rang the bell and waited.

A small pale man with a wrinkled forehead emerged from the back and placed two small thin hands flat on the counter. His face carried no discernible expression and Frank was reminded of a timid nocturnal creature disturbed from its resting-place. He

12

thought: If this is their idea of a warm welcome I'd hate to be around when they're positively indifferent.

The clerk's voice was as drab and unwelcoming as his manner.

"What can I do for you?"

"This is a hotel?" Frank said.

The clerk nodded.

"And you have vacancies?"

The clerk nodded again.

"I'd like to register."

"Have you made a reservation?"

Frank regarded the small pale man, who seemed quite serious, and blinked once or twice in mild surprise and with a growing sense of impatience.

"No, I haven't made a reservation. But if you have vacancies . . ."

"We have vacancies, as I've already told you," said the clerk, "but it's customary to book in advance. It's management policy here at the Cascade."

"Well I'm sorry about that," Frank said. "Next time I'll remember." He stood his ground and looked at the clerk's pale wrinkled forehead in the dimness; even now the man seemed hesitant to offer him a room and for a moment Frank experienced the crazy notion that they were going to stand facing one another until the light completely drained from the room. It was like a dream in which the simplest, most commonplace act is impossible to accomplish.

At last the clerk made a move and abruptly swivelled the register and held out a leaky ballpen. Frank saw that it had stained the man's fingers and used his own to sign his name and home address. The clerk reached behind him for a key and at the same time said in his flat, slightly nasal voice, "You're from Chicago."

It seemed neither a question nor a statement, and whatever it was Frank felt no obligation to respond. He picked up the key, glanced at the number on the metal tag, and dropped it into his pocket.

The clerk said, "Is it just for the one night?"

Frank picked up his leather suitcase. He faced the man and said, "More than likely. But if it isn't I'll let you know." His impatience had fed a slow burning annoyance, fanned by this churlish reception, and he didn't see why he should placidly answer the man's questions and volunteer any more information than was strictly required by law. They had his name and home address; they could whistle for the rest.

He went to an open staircase with curving oak banisters and paused before he mounted the first step, aware that the clerk was still watching him.

"I take it you have a dining room in this establishment."

The man's pale thin face nodded slowly in the dimness.

"And a bar?"

"Same place. Dining room opens at seven and you can get a drink there too."

"Thank you," Frank said, trying to keep the irony out of his voice.

"One second."

Frank turned at the bend in the staircase and supported himself with an outstretched arm against the bannister. "What is it?"

"You didn't ask the price of the room."

"I imagine I can afford it. And I have an American Express card if I run short."

"Fifteen dollars a night," the clerk informed him stonily.

"That's with breakfast."

"Without."

It was more than such a hotel was entitled to ask, but Frank didn't feel like arguing. He had his mind on the shower, the stiff drink, the meal. Perhaps later, or in the morning, he would feel angry about it, but just now he wasn't in the mood to haggle with a desk clerk who looked prematurely aged. In any case it was probably the only hotel in Gypsum, which was why they had the nerve to charge so much.

After the shower he felt better, and after the first drink better still. His preference was Southern Comfort, without ice or water, and he was glad to see the barman (who was also the waiter) pour him a generous measure. It was eight o'clock when he got around to eating, by which time darkness had descended on the town, the street outside lit by a few rather faint lamps which if anything seemed to intensify the blackness and the vivid night sky, spangled with sharp icy stars.

Of course, Frank thought, we're over a mile above sea level here. The air is thinner and there's less atmospheric disturbance. And with the mountain ranges encircling them the usual gentle mid-Western sunsets would be blocked out. It really gave him a feeling of being cut off, out here in the middle of the continent surrounded by walls of granite several miles thick. It was hardly surprising that the people exhibited an insularity of character when their entire lives were spent in such remote isolation.

The steak was good, thick and juicy, and the coffee

strong and black. He mellowed a little in his appraisal of the place and lit a cigarette to round off the meal. It was his ninth of the day—yet another attempt to break himself of the habit by strictly rationing his intake. The penalty of a desk job and especially that of being a writer when the mind is scrabbling for a thought decent enough to clothe with words.

The difference between himself and a journalist, as Frank Kersh was always too ready to point out, was that for a journalist the stories neatly categorized themselves and could almost be written off the top of his head. But articles and features dealing with difficult and complex scientific concepts—which comprised Frank's daily grind—had each to be approached individually and given the right sort of treatment. *Science Now* wasn't an abstruse technical journal filled with learned university papers, like say *Nature* or *Physics Review*, but was aimed at a broader readership which encompassed graduates, students and the intelligent lay reader. His training in biochemistry was useful but all the same he was expected to grapple with cosmology, astrophysics, quantum mechanics and a host of other scientific disciplines which no one man could be expected to master.

Even so, he prided himself on having achieved sufficient grounding in all the main categories to be able to hold a creditable conversation at a fairly high level. And when he wasn't sure he made a point of asking.

From his corner table in the small dining room he could see through into the lobby, which in the last ten to fifteen minutes had filled up; pink frosted wall lamps threw a soft glow over a small crowd of people, including the cowboy in his white Stetson and shiny spurs. There were cattle ranches hereabouts, Frank knew, and he guessed that the man must be the genuine article and not a drugstore dude.

He called the barman-waiter across, a young man in his twenties with a prominent sunburnt nose and a jutting Adam's apple which seemed to complement it, and asked what was going on.

"Reg'lar meetin'," said the young man, who had an exaggerated drawl which sounded in Frank's ears like an impersonation of a youthful Jimmy Stewart. "Folks come into town to listen to the preacher. He whips 'em up, they get drunk, fight a little, then sleep it off. Gettin' to be two, three times a week recently."

"You mean to say it's a Prayer Meeting?" Frank said, still not sure that he understood.

"Guess so." The young man nodded and wiped his large red knuckly hands on his apron. "Guess you could call it that."

"And they hold the meeting right here in the lobby?"

The young man shook his head. "Naw, they get together here to wait for the preacher, Mr. Cabel. He ain't got no reg'lar place to preach, so's they wait here till he gits hisself all fixed up in the street. Then the proceedin's commence.'

He pronounced it *co-mmence*.

Frank had heard how some of the small mid-West communities went in strongly for religious meetings, still carrying on the traditions of the fire-and-brimstone preachers who had wandered the country at the turn of the century, but it seemed odd that red-necked ranchers, farmers and mineworkers should be such

17

devoted students of the good book. It only went to show that living in the city gave you a distorted perspective on what the rest of America was up to; for Frank Kersh it was like stepping back eighty years into the past.

He said, "What denomination does Mr. Cabel represent?"

The young man had absently picked up a knife from the table and was polishing it. "Calls hisself a member of the Telluric Faith. The folks round here don't seem to care what the hell he is so long as he preaches a good sermon. And Mr. Cabel sure does that well enough."

"Telluric?" Frank repeated. He took a sip of Southern Comfort. "Is that some local religious sect? I've never heard of it before."

"Somethin' to do with the earth," the young man advised him. "Mr. Cabel talks a lot about earth and fire and water—calls 'em the prime sources from which everything springs. Myself I don't know too much about it. I listen in now and then but it don't seem to make a heck of a lot of sense."

The lobby was now full and amongst the gathering Frank caught sight of the hotel clerk. His small thin figure and pale narrow face with its set of corrugated vee-shaped wrinkles seemed conspicuously out of place alongside the broad sunburned ranchers and miners. There were no women present.

"I see the desk clerk's a member of the congregation."

The young man snorted down his nose. "That's Stringer. He helps organize the meetings and goes

18

round with the plate. If you ask me he's the one behind all this."

"Behind all what?" Frank said curiously.

But the young man had moved away, still polishing the knife, as if he hadn't heard—or chose to ignore—Frank's question. There was a small bar with half a dozen bottles and some upturned glasses on a tray and he busied himself behind it, keeping his face averted.

After a moment he said, "Can I get you another drink, mister? I mean *sir*—they keep telling me I should call hotel guests *sir*."

"Unless they happen to be women."

The barman-waiter turned his prominent red nose in Frank's direction. "Huh?" he said, his expression blank.

"You don't get many customers in here."

"They'll be in later, after the meeting. We get pretty busy about ten onwards." He seemed willing to talk once again. "You prob'bly won't get much sleep, mister—*sir*—they go on drinkin' and yappin' till all hours, and here's me got to get up at five-thirty in the mornin'." He puckered his lips and thrust them forward in a comical expression of pained martyrdom. "An' Chuck's the worst one of all," he muttered, half to himself.

"I guess Chuck is the cowboy."

"That's right." The young man leaned his sharp elbows on the bar, his head sunk between his shoulders. "But don't let Chuck hear you call him that. Chuck Strang is a *rancher*. Runs a breeding herd of 600 head along by Roaring Fork there. The Lazy W Ranch."

19

"What does he get out of the Telluric Faith? Does it help fatten up his cattle?"

The young man's eyes shifted evasively and he traced the wet imprint of a glass on the bar-top with a bony finger. "No use askin' me. I just serve them beer and bourbon."

"You can serve me another Southern Comfort," Frank said. He looked toward the lobby and saw that the people were slowly filing outside. The preacher must have arrived and the meeting proper was about to begin. As if a light had suddenly gone on inside his head Frank realized the significance of the word Telluric: it derived from the Latin *tellus* meaning of or pertaining to the Earth. What were these people—Earth worshipers? In one way, he supposed, it did make a weird kind of sense. Miners spent their working lives underground, digging into the bowels of the earth, so it was logical that they had a certain kind of reverence for it. But as for actually worshiping the planet and making it the focus of their religious homage—no, that didn't seem to square with the miners he had met in the past, tough hard-working men who wouldn't take bullshit from anybody, much less a fire-breathing preacher who had invented his own screwball religion.

The young man set the drink down in front of him. He said, "You movin' on in the morning, mister?"

"Not right away." There had seemed more than just a casual inquiry in the young man's tone; or was he reading devious meanings into something that was innocent and blameless, himself affected by this strange cult he had stumbled across in the middle of nowhere? He thought with a flash of wry humor that

20

if they were of the Telluric faith they probably referred to themselves as Tellurians: inhabitants of the Earth.

The young man had remained at the table, apparently still waiting for an answer. He wrapped his large raw-boned hands in the folds of his apron, imitating the motion of wiping them, even though they were perfectly dry. Frank Kersh interpreted this as a sign of unease.

He said, not seeing why he should conceal anything, "I'm here on business. There's a scientific establishment in the area which I'm covering for my journal. I'm a science writer," he added, to forestall the inevitable query as to whether this meant he was a reporter. People didn't seem to understand or appreciate the difference anyway.

The young man moved slowly away. The information didn't seem to have registered, or at any rate hadn't produced a reaction, but Frank saw that he was mistaken when the young man said, "Does Stringer know why you're here?"

"You mean the desk clerk?"

"He's the owner of this place."

"No, I didn't tell him. He never asked and I don't see what business it is of his."

"Then I wouldn't, mister. Don't tell him."

Frank laughed. "You make it sound mysterious."

"I'm jus' saying: if he doesn't know, don't tell him."

"Doesn't he get along with the scientists working on the Deep Hole Project?"

"None of them do. No way."

"You mean the rest of the sect?"

"None of them," the young man repeated flatly.

He turned and said, "Is that the official name of that place—Deep Hole?"

"That's how it's known to other scientists. Its official designation is the Rocky Mountain Neutrino Astrophysical Research Station. Why should Stringer have anything against the people who work there? I shouldn't think he has a clue about what they're doing there."

"He doesn't need to know—what matters to Stringer and the others is where they've situated the damn thing."

"You mean an old abandoned working on the side of the mountain?"

"Right." The young man nodded emphatically. "The Telluride Mine."

"Is that what it was called before the Project took it over?"

"The oldest mine in this part of the Rockies, and the deepest so they say. Goes right back to the first rush in the 1850s when Colorado was opened up for the first time. Men been diggin' that mine for more than a hundred years, then the scientists move in and everythin' goes haywire—"

As if realizing that he was talking too much the young man turned away and went behind the bar; it almost seemed as if he needed to place a physical barrier between them.

Frank now saw, or thought he did, the connection which linked the religious following to the old mine working: the Telluric sect apparently regarded it as possessing special religious significance because of its name—which in fact, as he now recalled, was the description of an oxide of tellurium, a silvery-white

22

non-metallic element found in association with gold, silver and bismuth. In some weird and wonderful fashion the Tellurians had confused the Latin derivative *telluric*—meaning "of the earth"—with the mineralogists' name for a non-metallic oxide: *telluride*. It seemed plausible enough, though it never ceased to amaze him how the human race had this capacity for conjuring up out of thin air random figments of fantasy and building an entire structure of belief on the shiftiest of premises.

He smiled, wondering if the scientists over at Deep Hole knew of the rash of rumor, distrust and consternation they had caused by innocently choosing to install their neutrino detection equipment at the bottom of the deepest shaft in North America. That was the whole point of the operation, of course, shielding the perchloroethylene tanks from cosmic rays and other background "noise" with a mile-thick layer of solid rock so that only the elusive massless, uncharged neutrino travelling at the speed of light would get through. Every other particle known to science would be stopped dead in its tracks, with only the "ghost particle of the atom," as it had been called, completing the trip into the depths of the mine.

It would be unreasonable to expect the layman to understand the need for such a location; he would naturally assume that the scientists were actively seeking something deep below ground and not simply using the mountain as an efficient shielding device to prevent stray and unwanted nuclear interactions.

Frank said goodnight and took his drink up to his room. It was on the first floor overlooking the small main square. The dim street lights made pools of pale illumination, leaving murky areas of darkness which were filled with the murmur of low voices. Frank stared out but could see nothing, and after a few moments stripped down to his underclothes and lay on the bed, his drink near at hand, a pleasant drowsiness pressing down on his eyelids.

Now that he was alone he thought longingly of the girl he had met out on the Coast. She had been very good. It had been one of those instantaneous attractions—for both of them—and five hours after meeting her at a publisher's cocktail party they had wound up in her bed making very satisfactory love. Susan Cleeve, twenty-nine, small and dark with a sexy generous mouth she had known how to use. Divorced, living alone, an attractive independent woman with a lively mind and a desirable body . . .

He had fallen into a light doze, drifting along on the gentle waves of pleasant retrospection, and then became slowly aware of the sound of low monotonous chanting from the square below. The words were indistinct, lost in the constant drone of voices, but as his senses sharpened he picked out the odd phrase here and there which seemed to have the ring of Biblical quotation. There was something about " . . . and the flood was forty days upon the earth," and another chant, repeated over and over again, which went, " . . . and the waters prevailed and were increased greatly upon the earth."

The Tellurians, it appeared, were prophesying doom and destruction in the manner of the Flood as depicted in the Bible. Yet another sect who believed that the end was nigh.

Turning the light off and going quickly to the window, Frank looked down into the dark square. He could vaguely make out a group of people, the dim lamplight catching the outline of a face, the shape of a hand, and now that his eyes were accustomed to the gloom he could plainly see the white Stetson, a ghostly hat on the head of its invisible wearer.

The preacher, Mr. Cabel—if he was there, which Frank assumed he was—was lost in the darkness. The chanting went on, rising and falling in the mournful rhythm of a funereal dirge. It seemed odd, and rather eerie, to be witnessing such an event in what was after all the most technologically advanced country on the face of the earth—and in an age of scientific reason and enlightenment when the antiquated voodoo of religious ceremony had, supposedly, been swept away along with primitive superstition and the belief in spirits.

The chanting lulled Frank to sleep that night, but his dreams were filled with cataclysmic visions of torrents of rushing floodwater and mountains split asunder by thunderbolts from the heavens.

CHAPTER THREE

The drive out to the Deep Hole Project took forty minutes. He hadn't asked directions, surmising that somewhere along the road east of Gypsum there would be a bridge crossing the Eagle River, and from that point he would watch out for signposts.

Five miles out of town he came to the bridge, a single-span timber construction with room enough for only one vehicle at a time. There was no sign pointing the way to the Project, which struck him as odd. The main highway carried on along the northern bank of the river to the next town of Avon, and further on, Mintburn, Red Cliff, Breckenridge and Climax. Somewhere in that vicinity—about ten miles away, he reckoned—was the Great Eagle Dam, built in the sixties to supply the High Plains territory to the east of the Continental Divide. This was the farmland of the State, good rich soil robbed of the rainfall it required by the granite backbone of the Rockies which lifted the rain-bearing cloud from the west and claimed most of the water for its own mountain streams. So the Dam had been built to feed Denver and the vast flat acreage where crops were grown and the bulk of the cattle reared.

Beyond the bridge the road turned from smooth grey asphalt into red shale. It started to climb, gradually at first, past small rocky outcrops, then steepened and began to curl in a series of sharp hairpin loops. Below and to his left Frank could see the winding thread of the river, and further away a speckle of buildings which was Gypsum.

The Mount of the Holy Cross was immediately above him, so close that he couldn't get a good look at it. The weather at the moment was fine and clear, the temperature quite mild for the time of year, but he could easily imagine what it would be like when the snows came and blanketed the range, virtually sealing off the Project from the outside world. He wondered what they did in winter for supplies; if there was a suitable piece of flat ground it was possible that helicopters could maintain the supply-line, or maybe they stocked up for months ahead and sat it out—but it would be a bleak kind of existence, marooned up here on the side of the mountain.

Still no marker. This annoyed him a little and for a moment he thought he'd taken the wrong road; yet how could he lose his way when there was only a single track leading upward in ever-decreasing spirals? Most scientific establishments (except the top secret ones) were adequately sign-posted and there was no reason he could think of why Deep Hole shouldn't be the same.

The road levelled out and up ahead he could see three logs lashed together to form an entrance. Nailed to the one spanning the road there was a sign which read: Telluride Mine. This had to be the place. And then he did see a small metal plaque, no bigger than a letter-box, which as he drove slowly up to it transpired to have the words *US Institute of Astrophysics* stamped across its metal face, and below in smaller letters, *Solar Neutrino Research Station*.

Nothing like being ostentatious, Frank thought.

The prefabricated huts, half a dozen or so grouped together, were set some distance away across a compound of packed red earth from the mine-head, which itself was enclosed by a new brick building, the winding gear above contained in a latticework of steel girders painted bright orange. The authorities had obviously spent more on the equipment than on the living quarters, which Frank personally thought was a poor balance and bad psychology. The best equipment in the world wouldn't achieve results if the personnel who had to operate it were living in what they felt were below-standard conditions.

There were several people about but none of them paid any attention to him as he stepped out of the car and slung his Pentax camera and Plustron cassette recorder across his shoulder. He'd chosen to wear a short denim jacket and jeans, anticipating that part of the day would be spent scrambling in and out of a wire cage and travelling for periods underground. He hoped they wouldn't object to his taking photographs, which even if the editor decided not to use them were always useful as reference. Some scientists could be touchy about giving too much away, despite the fact that their particular line of work might be known and well-documented in umpteen scientific papers.

But Professor Friedmann raised no objection. He'd been given advance warning of the visit and seemed amenable to Frank's request to take shots of the underground installation. He was a tall spare man—in his mid-fifties, Frank guessed—with short grey hair that was razored in a line above his ears. He wore blue-tinted spectacles with metal frames which seemed to lend him a rather bemused attitude as if life's little surprises always took him aback slightly. He wasn't vague or absent-minded, yet there was almost a kind of innocence about him that reminded Frank of a brainy though naive schoolboy.

His greeting was cordial, if a little guarded, but then Frank Kersh was accustomed to the caution of scientists and academics when dealing with the press. They had it firmly fixed in their minds that he was "a reporter," and as such had to be treated with skepticism, if not open distrust.

"If you're looking for a 'scoop' I'm afraid you've come to the wrong place," said Professor Friedmann with forced joviality. "Isn't that what you fellows are always after, a new and exciting scientific 'breakthrough'?" He spoke the jargon words self-consciously, in the arch manner of an adult unused to conversing with children but making a gallant effort to do so.

"I'm with *Science Now*, not *Hustler*," Frank said with a smile. "Our editorial policy is to treat scientific and technical subjects with the degree of seriousness they deserve. But if you've made a breakthrough in neutrino astronomy I'd be happy to hear about it."

Professor Friedmann shook his head and indicated a foot-high pile of computer printout folded concertina-fashion on his desk. "There's our latest batch of data, three weeks' D and D processed and analyzed by computer. No surprises there I'm sorry to say."

"D and D?" Frank said, flipping open his notebook.

"Ah, yes. You're obviously not well-up in neutrino terminology." He cleared his throat, smiling gently. "Detection and Differentiation. It's a two-stage process whereby we have to observe the various particle interactions in the tanks and then interpret and classify each one. There are random events happening all the while, as I'm sure you'll appreciate, so it's essential to differentiate those from the neutrino interactions."

"The crucial factor being the rate and frequency at which chlorine-37 is transformed into argon-37."

Professor Friedmann's smile faded at the edges. "Then you do know something about neutrino detection?" He blinked behind his blue-tinted glasses and pinched his nostrils together with thumb and forefinger.

"Something," Frank agreed. "Not a great deal."

He had always found it best to underplay his hand in matters of scientific knowledge: in this way scientists tended to be more forthcoming and sometimes revealed information they otherwise might not have done.

"Well, as you may know, Mr. Kersh, our principle concern at Deep Hole is to detect and measure the number of neutrinos being emitted by the Sun's core. These are formed during the fusion of hydrogen to helium. It's been accurately estimated that during this process the Sun loses 4,600,000 tons of mass each second, which represents about 0.71 of the total mass of hydrogen being fused to helium, and from that we know that the total number of hydrogen nuclei being fused every second in the Sun is 3.6×10^{38} — or if you want it in round figures, 360,000,-

000,000,000,000,000,000,000,000,000,000,000."

His eyes narrowed behind the blue lenses, a mannerism which reminded Frank of a schoolmaster making sure his pupil had grasped what he was being taught.

"And from this we can estimate the number of neutrinos being produced each second in the Sun's core at 1.8×10^{38}, or in other words, 180,000,000,-000,000,000,000,000,000,000,000,000. Unlike photons, the particles of light and heat formed in the core, which take about a million years to reach the surface, the neutrino takes three seconds, and travelling at the speed of light reaches the Earth in eight minutes. Because it has no mass and no charge it passes through the Earth as if it were a cloud of gas, in about 1/125 of a second, and carries on into space. But very occasionally a neutrino will react with an atom of chlorine and this absorption forms argon atoms which, being radioactive, we can detect with our equipment."

"Is it known how many neutrinos reach the Earth from the Sun's core?"

Professor Friedmann nodded. "Oh yes, quite a simple calculation. Every second the Earth receives 80,000,000,000,000,000,000,000,000,000, neutrinos from the Sun. Every square centimeter of the Earth's cross-section receives about 60,000,000,000 neutrinos each second." He smiled briefly. "It's quite interesting to note that every second of the day and night we are being bombarded by several billion neutrinos which pass clean through us as if we didn't exist."

"Perhaps just as well," Frank said. "I'd hate to think of what might happen if they decided to interact with interact with some of my atoms."

"Not possible," Professor Friedmann said shortly, as if taking Frank's comment seriously. "There's no evidence at all to suggest that neutrinos in any way affect human beings."

He went on to talk about the processing of data, which Frank was surprised to learn was carried out by the computer facility at NORAD, the North American Air Defense Command which was situated inside Cheyenne Mountain, about sixty miles away, south of Colorado Springs. The NORAD Combat Operations Center was built inside the mountain itself, under a granite roof a quarter-mile thick and behind 30-ton blastproof doors.

"I assumed their computer time would be fully taken up with their own data processing requirements," Frank said.

"They have three systems, two of which are on-line at any one moment, so they have spare capacity available which we're free to use."

"And these are the data you've just received," Frank said, reaching out to the printout.

Professor Friedmann laid his hand on the pile. "Yet to be checked and verified," he said. "But you can take my word that there's nothing out of the ordinary here. Our present detection rate is one neutrino a month, which is consistent with other findings to date."

"One neutrino out of 60 billion per square centimeter—wouldn't you expect more?"

"Well, yes, we would," Professor Friedmann admitted. He stood up, seeming rather agitated. "We can only assume that our methods are nowhere near as efficient as they ought to be. I take it you'd like to see the installation for yourself, Mr. Kersh. You'll excuse me if I don't accompany you, but my assistant, Dr. Leach, is already below ground and he'll be happy to answer any questions you might have."

Frank took this to be a polite way of terminating the interview. It seemed that while Friedmann was quite willing to discuss the theoretical background to solar neutrino detection he was reluctant to go into specific details concerning the Project's research program and its record of success—or lack of it. Perhaps he was afraid that the US Institute of Astrophysics would reduce the budget or cancel it altogether if word got around that the detection rate was a single paltry neutrino every thirty days.

The cage was a solid aluminum box without windows, large enough to accommodate a dozen people, and dropping down a mile-deep shaft at twenty-two feet per second gave Frank the unnerving feeling of being in free fall. When they reached the bottom it took him several moments to regain his composure and recover his stomach, which had followed at a more sedate pace. The young technical assistant who accompanied him ducked his head aside and grinned, enjoying the expression of Frank's face; Frank debated with himself whether he should throw up as well, just to make the young man's day.

As he stepped out his breath was literally taken away. There was a steady warm breeze blowing in his face which was tainted with the smell of diesel oil and something more pungent that he couldn't identify. Except for the powerful odor it might have been a warm summer wind blowing along the main tunnel. He said:

33

"Air conditioning?" and the technical assistant nodded, sliding the aluminum door shut behind him.

"The air's so sluggish down here we've got to keep a fresh supply coming in and constantly on the move. And it helps to clear the stink of the solution."

"That's right. You've got a lot of perchloroethylene down here."

"Four tanks each containing 150,000 gallons of the stuff. Any spots or stains you want cleaning off?"

This was a reference to the other more common use of perchloroethylene—as a dry-cleaning fluid. It was exactly the same chemical composition as the fluid which could be bought in any hardware store, the important thing being that it contained two carbon atoms and four chlorine atoms, the chlorine absorbing a neutrino to become an argon atom.

The neutrino really was a ghost particle. Its name derived from the Italian *neutrino*, meaning "little neutral one," proposed by the Italian physicist Enrico Fermi. The existence of such a particle had been postulated back in the thirties by Wolfgang Pauli to maintain the laws of the conservation of energy, but it wasn't till the mid-fifties that specific experimental evidence was forthcoming that the particle had actually been detected. And its elusiveness wasn't all that surprising when you considered that, on average, a neutrino would have to travel through 3,500 light-years of solid matter—something as dense as lead—before hitting and interacting with another particle. So even allowing for the fact that billions and billions of neutrinos were passing through the Earth every second it perhaps wasn't to be wondered at that an infinitesimal percentage of them was detected in the tanks.

Yet if this were so, why was Friedmann unhappy about discussing his results in detail? Had he discovered fresh evidence about solar neutrinos that he was unwilling to reveal, or was he trying to hide a paucity of hard factual data with bland assurances that the detection rate was "consistent with other findings to date?" Frank Kersh couldn't figure it out; it was a tiny yet irritating puzzle whose solution eluded him.

They rode in a small fiberglass cab along an electrified track, moving at a steady fifteen miles an hour along the main illuminated gallery before turning into a smaller, darker tunnel which seemed to curve and descend deeper, though it was difficult to estimate distance and orientation because there were no points of reference with which to judge their progress. The tunnel became narrower still, the two powerful lights mounted on the roof of the cab probing the blank walls ahead, and it seemed to Frank that they had travelled a considerable distance. He asked the technical engineer which direction they were headed in and how much further they had to go.

"Nearly two miles from the shaft to the installation, which is slap-bang under the mountain. So you're not only a mile underground, you've got another 14,000 feet of solid rock on top of that. That way the Professor figures we screen out most of the background radiation—gamma rays, x-rays and so on —and anything that gets through all that can only be our little elusive friend."

Frank stared ahead into the twin circles of light bouncing against the roof and walls. On the floor of the tunnel he could see reflected the single steel track, like a smooth shiny metal ribbon vanishing into the blackness.

He said, "How many people do you have working on the Project?"

"Upwards of twenty. There are eighteen of us in the research team, including the Professor and Dr. Leach, and half-a-dozen engineers who look after the mine and see that the winding gear is properly maintained."

"No women?"

The technical assistant shook his head ruefully. "No women."

"What's your function?"

"I work with Dr. Leach. He's in charge of the detection equipment underground, so we operate a shift roster with four men permanently on duty. Gets to be pretty boring except for once a week when we flush the tanks with helium; that's to collect any argon-37 present which we then run a radioactive count on."

"And how's it been going?"

The technical assistant turned his head and looked directly at him. Frank thought for a moment that he wasn't going to answer, but then he said, "Didn't Professor Friedmann give you the figures?"

"He said there were no surprises."

"That's it," said the technical assistant, looking ahead once more. "No surprises."

The tunnel opened out and Frank was momentarily dazzled by a bank of lights in the roof of an enormous chamber, as wide and high as the main hall at Grand Central Station. Four huge stainless steel tanks about twenty feet high were cemented into the floor, arranged in line one after the other, a series of silver-coated pipes connecting them and running into what appeared to be a filtration apparatus mounted on a concrete base. The smell of perchloroethylene was very strong now, stinging the nostrils and making Frank's eyes fill with moisture.

The technical assistant laughed. "You get used to it after a while. And it sure clears up any sinus trouble you might have."

Frank sneezed and wiped his eyes. He was beginning to find the technical assistant's sense of humor a little wearing.

The cab had halted in a siding and they climbed out and walked past the tanks to a two-story steel gantry where three men were sitting within an arrangement of consoles and instrumentation, elevated above the floor of the cavern. Two of the men were fairly young, in their twenties; the third was older, Frank presumed, though it was difficult to tell; he was a dwarf.

As they reach the top of the metal stairway the technical assistant said in an undertone. "Dr. Leach isn't too sociable. He doesn't think visitors should be allowed down here. So I'd be careful what I asked him if I were you."

It was oppressively warm and Frank was sweating. The breeze was gentler here than in the tunnels and the humidity very high, the body perspiring while at rest without even expending any effort.

The technical assistant introduced Mr. Kersh from *Science Now* and Dr. Leach's bulbous eyes passed hurriedly and rather impatiently across Frank's face, seeming to take him in and dismiss him in a

37

single brief glance. He didn't offer his hand but said at once in a voice that was low and throaty, almost a growl, "We're extremely busy, I hope Professor Friedmann told you that. We haven't got time to answer journalists' questions when we're conducting important scientific research."

He crouched rather than sat on the chair, his feet not touching the floor, and there was something even more strange about him that Frank at first didn't comprehend: then he realized what it was: although his head and shoulders and arms were those of a normal-sized man the rest of his body appeared to have shrunk or wasted away so that his deformity was made even more grotesque by the ungainly joining of ill-matched parts. He was half-man, half-dwarf, the cruellest of nature's jokes in combining odd bits and pieces left over from other human beings.

Frank said, "I'll try not to take up too much of your time, Dr. Leach. But if I might correct you on one point: I'm a science writer, not a journalist."

"Is that a camera you've got there?" Dr. Leach said pettishly. "You're not to take any photographs, I hope that's clearly understood."

"Professor Friedmann raised no objection."

"Professor Friedmann isn't in charge of the installation; I am. The Professor is Project leader but I'm responsible for everything below ground."

Frank nodded slowly. "I see."

He also saw that he wasn't going to impress Dr. Leach with his charm, tact and good manners. The man had made up his mind and there didn't appear to be much hope of changing it; in any case Frank didn't feel too strong an inclination to try. It seemed that the scientists on the Deep Hole Project had buried themselves out of sight of civilization in more than just the geographical sense.

"Did you bring the photographic plates with you, Fawbert?" Dr. Leach said, addressing the technical assistant.

"Williams is bringing them down on the second period."

"I wanted them for midday," Dr. Leach said, swivelling around on his chair. "I expressly asked for them to be brought down within the hour." He gripped the arms of the chair, his hands large and heavily veined, covered in dark hair, and levered himself to the floor. The top of his head came no higher than Frank's chest. "You'll have to return to the surface and get them."

He went across to a bank of instrumentation and walked along looking closely at each dial, which were level with his face. Frank was reminded of a surly precocious child examining a birthday train set to ensure that all the parts were in good working order.

Fawbert released a small sigh and glanced at one of the other technicians. The man shrugged and made a face. Frank thought: One big happy family. Snow White and the seven . . .

He unslung his camera and cassette recorder and went to stand at the rail, the huge rectangular stainless steel tanks seen in acute perspective from this vantage point. High above in the roof of the chamber the battery of lights illuminated everything with a harsh bleakness, like a football stadium at night. At his elbow Fawbert said quietly:

"I did mention there might be a small problem with Dr. Leach."

Frank grunted and took out a pack of cigarettes.

The technical assistant shook his head. "Smoking isn't allowed. Fire risk."

"Is he going to talk to me, do you think?"

"He might do." Fawbert swept a frond of fair hair out of his eyes. "Sometimes he can be okay, but just at the moment . . ."

"What's happening at the moment?"

"Nothing special. I didn't mean it that way." Fawbert glanced over his shoulder. "You can never tell with him; I think maybe it's the physical thing. He's dedicated himself to the Project and he gets uptight if outsiders start butting in. I guess it's understandable."

"But not very sociable."

Dr. Leach had returned to his desk and Frank strolled across. He waited a moment, studying the lowered head of thick black hair, before saying, "I wonder if you've any comment to make on the USSR gallium-germanium detector, Dr. Leach? The first results are expected any day now. Do you think they'll add significantly to our knowledge of solar neutrina flux?"

The scientist completed the notation he was making and slowly raised his head. His eyes were a deep dark brown, almost black, the brows a thick dark bar across his forehead. He said, "The Soviets are investigating a different energy band to ourselves. They're hoping to detect neutrinos of less than 0.4 million electron volts. Our energy spectrum is much higher."

"Above 5 million electron volts."

Dr. Leach regarded him with a fixed intensity that was not so much hostile as wary and suspicious. Then he said, "That is correct. In excess of 5 million electron volts. The Soviet findings will no doubt prove useful but they do not affect our research directly. In a sense they complement—"

Apparently he had heard something, for he cocked his head to one side, and then Frank heard it too: a subdued moaning in the far distance, sounding like the bleak wailing of a prairie wind, or a beast in pain trapped in the bowels of the earth. It might have been his imagination (he wasn't sure) but Frank also thought he felt a tremor pass through the soles of his feet, a low-frequency vibration which seemed to jar the fillings in his teeth.

He looked questioningly at the others, who had frozen in attitudes of listening, and then his attention was caught and held by the expression on Dr. Leach's face. He had seen people under hypnosis and the scientist reminded him of someone in a state of trance, lost to this world and inhabiting a region beyond the normal senses, where the private inner visions of the mind constitute the single ultimate reality.

CHAPTER FOUR

Walt Stringer, manager of the Cascade Hotel, closed the roll-top desk and went to answer the ping of the bell. It had to be the stranger, no doubt about it, because the locals either called out his name or came directly into the office. It was him, all right, his vivid blue eyes and brown curly hair marking him out as quite a youngish man until you got closer and saw the delta of creases at the corners of his eyes and the slight heaviness in the line of the jaw. And he had thickened up around the waist—a sure sign of age, more than moderate drinking, and soft city living. Stringer had hoped to have seen the last of him and here he was again, his leather grip in his hand and an assortment of gear slung across his shoulder.

As Stringer came out of the office, closing the door behind him, Frank Kersh said, "You don't face too much competition for accommodation in this town."

"What's wrong, don't you like our hospitality?"

"Your food's okay and your liquor's fine; it's the fifteen dollar cover charge that's a little steep. It isn't as though there was a private bathroom."

"Don't see as how that's necessary," Stringer

42

answered. "One bathroom on every floor. Should be enough for most folks' needs."

"You can put me down for another fifteen dollars' worth."

"I thought you were moving on—don't they need you on your paper back in Chicago?"

Frank slowly smiled. "Did I mention I was a journalist?"

"You got a PA sticker on your windshield, ain't you?" Stringer said, reaching before him for the key.

It was true—though not many people recognized the Press Association symbol when they saw it. He hadn't intented to return to Gypsum, only it was late afternoon when he had finally left the Project and he didn't feel in the mood for a long drive. He reasoned that it was better to spend the night locally and make an early start in the morning: a day's hard driving should see him safely back in the Windy City.

He was given the same room, overlooking the main square. After a shower he sat down to write up his notes, listening to the interview he had taped with Professor Friedmann, though it was plainly unsatisfactory in the way of providing fresh information. It seemed that Perry had been right in his estimation of the Deep Hole Project; not expecting very much and having his judgment confirmed. Listening to it over again it sounded less like an interview than a first-term college lecture.

Frank had used the notebook technique before. He didn't regard it as outright deception, simply a trick of the trade to get his subject talking more freely. His method was to start the recorder before the interview and then pretend to take notes so that the interviewee was relaxed, unaware that he was being taped. It had been his experience that some people froze at the sight of a microphone and became tongue-tied.

Shortly before eight he went down to the dining room and sat at the same table, the young barman-waiter lifting his elbows off the bar and bringing him a Southern Comfort without being asked. His name, Frank learned, was Spencer Tutt. He seemed less guarded than he had the previous evening and when Frank invited him to have a drink he accepted, pouring himself a Schlitz and raising his glass. After the first swallow he said in his drawling voice, "Old man Stringer was askin' about you. Seems he cottoned on that you was a reporter. Only I didn't tell him," he added quickly.

"I'm not ashamed of the fact. Why do you suppose he's interested in me?"

Spencer Tutt shrugged his lean shoulders. "Guess he knew you had somethin' to do with what's goin' on over at the Telluride Mine."

"How could he know that?"

"You weren't here on vacation, that was pretty obvious, so maybe he figured it out for hisself. And when you came back you had red mud on your tires. That means you must have taken the mountain road over Eagle River."

"Mr. Stringer is a regular Sherlock Holmes," Frank said. He was about to ask if the earth tremor had been felt in Gypsum but something restrained him. The memory brought with it the association of Dr. Leach, the strange dwarfish man whose dark fixed stare had almost seemed to contain an element of madness, and it was a recollection that Frank wasn't keen to dwell upon. Perhaps it wasn't so surprising that the townspeople regarded the scientific community with suspicion and distrust.

He ordered steak, spinach and salad, apple pie and cream, black coffee, and about halfway through the meal three or four people drifted in and sat down. By the look of them they were farmhands, wearing faded blue overalls, their faces and arms burned a rich mahogany by spending most of the working day outdoors. Frank scrutinized them casually, wondering if any of them had been present at the Prayer Meeting the night before, but he couldn't recall their faces with any degree of certainty.

He finished his meal and had decided to have one more Southern Comfort before going up to his room when a short, broad, balding man in a wrinkled white cotton suit entered and made unsteadily for the bar. A couple of the farmhands greeted him, then glanced at one another with the secret amused air of people sharing a private joke.

Frank thought: Wherever you go you run across them—sometimes literally—the town drunk. This, by the look of it, was Gypsum's contribution to the national alcoholic problem. He watched as the man leaned heavily against the bar, his short stubby legs braced apart for stability, his creased cotton jacket riding up over the broad swell of his buttocks. Spencer Tutt served him with a bourbon and water and the man turned to survey the room, clutching the glass, his eyes shifting vaguely and near-sightedly over the half-dozen people seated at the tables; no one paid any attention to him, and after gulping down most of his drink he set off in Frank Kersh's general direction.

Frank fervently hoped that this wasn't going to be another tedious encounter with a screwball. His largely wasted day at the Deep Hole Project hadn't left him sufficient reserves of the milk of human kindness to suffer the incoherent ramblings of a down-and-out lush. But in this he was mistaken, for as the man approached him, managing somehow to avoid stumbling into tables and chairs, there seemed to be a definite sense of purpose in his movements, and his eyes too had sharpened into focus, losing their hazy meandering blankness.

He halted and bowed rather clumsily, raising his glass in a gesture of friendly introduction. The breast-pocket of his jacket was stained with ink, Frank noticed, as if from a leaky pen, and there was a bundle of papers sticking out of his pocket. In a voice that was surprisingly firm and under control he said:

"I believe we're in the same line of business. Cal Renfield, editor of the *Roaring Fork Bulletin*, what you'd call the local rag. Mind if I sit?"

He had already pulled out a chair and maneuvered his bulk into position, and without waiting for a response lowered himself carefully so that his belly came to rest on his upper thighs. He released a long deep sigh and closed his eyes, taking a swig and setting the glass down.

"Frank Kersh," Frank said sociably, somewhat relieved that the short fat man wasn't a free-loader. Or so he hoped. He said, "I'm not with a newspaper myself—"

"I know," Cal Renfield said at once, nodding briskly. He wiped his head which had a bald strip down the center and grey thinning hair either side, with a square plump hand, and then looked intently at the tips of his fingers. "Humidity's higher than hell tonight. Must be a thunderstorm on the way. Wind from the south and that's usually a bad sign."

Frank studied him circumspectly, looking for signs of chronic drunkenness, the trembling hands, the uncontrollable nervous tics in the facial muscles, the patchwork of crazed skin on the nose and cheeks where hundreds of tiny blood-vessels had fractured and burst; yet Cal Renfield exhibited none of these symptoms. Perhaps he just went on the occasional blinder, making up for all the other times when he stayed hard-headed and stone cold sober.

As if reading his thoughts Cal Renfield swayed forward a little and said in a confidential whisper, "You caught me on a bad day, Mr. Kersh. 'Bout once a month I take it into my head to—" he waved his well-padded hands about as if groping for words "—you, know, dip my head in the bucket and forget the paper, the town, the whole damn thing. Tomorrow I'm gonna be sorry but tonight is worth it."

"Can you stand another?" Frank asked, smiling. "Try me."

Frank nodded toward Spencer Tutt and the young man winked and set up some fresh glasses.

"You're with a science magazine, right?" Cal Renfield said, lacing his podgy fingers across his belly.

"Based in Chicago."

"And you've been out to the Project at the old Telluride working."

Frank shrugged. "So everybody seems to know. Is there bad feeling between the scientists and the townspeople? Don't they get on?"

"What makes you ask that?"

"The general feeling about the place. I get the impression that the townspeople don't understand what's going on at the Project and they're naturally suspicious when a bunch of scientists move in and start installing equipment underground. Most small communities would react the same way."

Spencer Tutt brought the drinks to the table and Cal Renfield took a hefty swallow before considering his reply. He put the glass down and relaced his fingers across his paunch. "It amounts to more than mere suspicion, Mr. Kersh."

"You're going to tell me that the Telluric Faith or whatever it calls itself has received some Divine intimation of disaster. They were performing outside the hotel last night: cheap theatricals to scare the locals."

"So you heard them?"

"I had no option."

"And you weren't impressed."

Frank raised his eyebrows. "With primitive mumbo-jumbo?" He shook his head.

"I forgot—you're a scientist yourself."

"A science writer. But you're not going to tell me that you believe their nonsense? You don't look to me like a man who's taken in by a bunch of people chanting a few Biblical quotes."

"No I'm not. When I said there was more to it than mere suspicion I wasn't thinking of Cabel and his followers. Other things have been happening round here lately that I can't explain and I doubt if anyone can." His eyes glazed over for a moment as if the alcohol had suddenly begun to affect him, then he seemed to shake himself out of it. "You ever been in this part of the world before, Mr. Kersh? Know anything of its history?"

"It was once gold-mining territory about a hundred years ago."

"That's right. Colorado was opened up by the prospectors back in the 1860s and a lot of men made their fortunes here. I wasn't thinking of that so much as how these mountains came to be formed—eighty, ninety million years ago. Ever heard of a woman called Helen Hunt Jackson? She lived around here at the end of the last century, studied these mountains and wrote about them. In one of her books she said: 'The weirdest of places with rocks of every conceivable and inconceivable shape and size, all motionless and silent, with a strange look of having been just stopped and held back in the very climax of some supernatural catastrophe.' I think she described this part of the Rockies pretty well. Wouldn't you say so?"

Frank nodded and took a sip of Southern Comfort. "There are some weird rock formations around here, I'll grant you that. But what has that got to do with the scientists working at the Deep Hole Project? Or why the townspeople distrust them?"

"I'll tell you why," said Cal Renfield, easing himself forward and placing his elbows on the checkered tablecloth. His face was round and bland, the features molded like soft wax, and it might have been a comical face but for his eyes which were grey, shrewd, intelligent—despite their occasional glazed wandering. "Some of the people around here—and not only those of the Telluric Faith—believe that when Helen

Hunt Jackson used the phrase 'supernatural catastrophe' she wasn't being fanciful or poetic but stating a historical fact. They really believe the rocks to be haunted, to have some inner dynamic power which is waiting to be released. There are too many tales the old miners used to tell of strange things happening underground: rocks moving without cause, shafts opening and closing mysteriously, lights from nowhere moving about in the darkness. You're new to this area, Mr. Kersh, so you don't know the historical background against which these people have been brought up. It's easy for an outsider to sneer and call their beliefs primitive and naive but you haven't had any first-hand experience with these mountains." He jerked a broad flat thumb over his shoulder. "And especially that one."

"The Mount of the Holy Cross?"

Cal Renfield threw back the last of his drink. He put the glass down and wiped his mouth. "Whether they knew it or not those scientists picked the one spot which is the focal point for what the locals regard as the most sacred *and* the most mysterious part of the mountain . . . the Telluride Mine. You can call it superstition if you want to but there aren't many along Roaring Fork Valley who don't believe in it."

"They think the mine is haunted?" Frank said. His expression must have been one of amused skepticism, for Cal Renfield said with a flash of annoyance:

"Science can't explain everything and the man who says it can is a fool."

"I wouldn't dispute that. Any good scientist knows that his knowledge is far outweighed by his ignorance. But there's a hell of a difference between belief and superstition on the one hand and hard scientific evidence on the other. You're not saying that we should credit every crackpot story with being the absolute, incontrovertible truth? There has to be some sort of proof, some objective evidence that we can look at dispassionately and examine as rational human beings—"

"What about the irrational, the inexplicable?" Cal Renfield said. His face was bathed in a light sheen of perspiration which had gathered in droplets in the folds under his eyes. Frank was also aware that it had become much warmer in the room, the atmosphere heavy and humid. Cal Renfield was about to go on when he noticed that his glass was empty. He raised his arm and snapped his fingers, which was evidently a signal that Spencer Tutt had been trained to respond to—fresh drinks were already on their way.

Frank Kersh ruffled his curly hair and stretched himself. He was beginning to feel the liquor creeping up from his gut and making dizzying spirals inside his head; another couple of shots and he'd be under the table himself.

He said, "Look, Mr. Renfield, I don't—"

"Call me Cal, for chrissakes. We're getting smashed together. What better basis for a friendly relationship?" He sucked eagerly at his glass.

"I wouldn't dispute there's a lot we don't understand, Cal. Hell, that's what science is all about, exploring the unknown, investigating the cosmos, delving into the sub-microscopic world of the atom. But at the same time we have to use our minds and not just accept things in terms of blind belief. If there was any concrete evidence that something strange was happening in connection with the Project I'd be the first to listen—all you've fed me so far are miners' tales from a hundred years ago."

Cal Renfield nodded. He was about to say something and a bubble of wind got in the way. When it had cleared he said, "All right, you want proof. I'll give you some. The Project started up two years ago. Since that time the weather around here has gone haywire—don't take my word for it, check the records. We've had more electrical thunderstorms recorded over a fourteen-month period than in the previous five years. And that is *fact.*"

"The freak weather conditions might be fact but who's to say that the Project is in any way responsible?" Frank demanded. "You're making an arbitrary assumption that the one caused the other; maybe it did but there's no evidence to prove it." His eyes were bright and blue, enlivened by the alcohol and the argument; he decided that he liked Cal Renfield but it still irritated him when intelligent people allowed their irrational fears and prejudices to overrule their basic common sense. Why couldn't they see that the truth could only be arrived at through a process of calm, logical deduction, casting aside subjective feelings and unreliable emotions?

He said in a quiet even voice, "Listen, Cal, let me tell you what the scientists at the Deep Hole Project are trying to do. There's a species of sub-atomic particle called the neutrino which originates in the Sun's core. As soon as it's formed it shoots out into space at the speed of light and some of these particles reach Earth. Most of them—the vast majority of them in fact—go straight through and out the other side in a fraction of a second, but now and then, very occasionally, a neutrino will interact with another particle and that's how we know it's there. At this instant there are thousands of neutrinos passing through our bodies but we're unaware of them; as far as they're concerned we hardly exist. Don't you see? The Deep Hole Project is a passive experiment, its only function is to detect neutrinos, calculate their velocity, and in this way we hope to get some idea of what's happening in the innermost depths of the Sun. And all this isn't vague supposition or blind belief, it's proven scientific fact."

Cal Renfield had listened to this, staring at the red and white checkered tablecloth, and now he raised his head and regarded Frank with those grey shrewd eyes of his. He said presently, "The entire Earth is being bombarded with these particles?"

Frank nodded. "That's right. Every thing and every body."

"So how do we know they aren't affecting us?"

Frank smiled and placed his hands flat on the table. "Because there's no evidence to suggest that. Quite the reverse in fact. Neutrinos are like ghost particles, with no mass and no charge. To them we're as nebulous as a patch of hazy gas floating about in space. They pass through us like a high-velocity bullet going through thin air."

"Then how come they can detect them at the bottom of a mine shaft one mile underground?"

"They've installed tanks of liquid which occasionally trap a neutrino. It's as simple as that. Neutrinos have been passing through these mountains since the day they were formed; it's unlikely they're going to set up some sort of strange nuclear interaction after

53

eighty million years, and there's no reason why they should."

Cal Renfield sniffed and studied his glass. He seemed to be debating something with himself, his lower lip thrust out, and then he said, "You pride yourself on being a hard-headed realist, Frank, a rational man. How would you explain what's been happening to the kids born around here over the past fourteen months or so? One in three has shown signs of abnormal development: how does your scientific mind cope with that?"

He looked up and his eyes were flat and hard; perspiration gleamed in the creases on his neck and the collar of his shirt was a dark ring.

Frank said, "Are you serious? Abnormal in what way?"

"They don't behave like newborn babies," Cal Renfield said in a low voice. "They don't respond to external stimuli. They don't cry and it doesn't seem to bother them if they're fed or not. They grow but they don't develop—is that abnormal enough for you?" His voice had risen and the room had gone quiet, the farmhands motionless and attentive, watching.

Frank said, "There must be a medical explanation for what's happened. If it's confined to this area there could be a virus going around, or maybe the ante-natal care was at fault in some way—"

"Then you talk to the medics yourself," Cal Renfield told him. "I have and I've gotten nowhere fast. Some of those babies are over a year old now and the doctors still don't know what's the matter with them or what they ought to do about it . . . so

54

much for the wonders of medical science."

Frank was puzzled and intrigued and was about to press Cal Renfield for more details when his attention was caught by a girl standing at the entrance to the dining room. Before he had time to register anything more than a broad fleeting impression she had reached their table and was standing above them with one hand resting aggressively on her hip and the other poking into the wrinkled cotton sleeve of Cal Renfield's jacket, her sharp pointed nails digging into his arm.

"So you had some proofs to check, did you? Work piled up at the office and you had to clear it before morning. I've had dinner waiting for two hours and all along you're sitting here getting sozzled with any bum who's willing to listen to you for the price of a drink."

Cal Renfield's eyes were shut tight. His face had adopted an expression of pained and weary martyrdom; then he opened the eye nearest to Frank and squinted at him in hopeless defeat.

Frank Kersh thought it wise not to say anything.

"Okay, okay," said Cal Renfield, raising his square podgy hands. "I told a white lie. I'm a bad little boy. Spank me and send me to bed without any supper."

He looked at Frank and nodded his head toward the girl. "My daughter, Helen," he said in the tone of a man apologizing for a tiresome maiden aunt who's decided to break up a poker school. "She feels responsible for me."

The girl, red-haired, slim, with nothing about her to suggest that she was Renfield's daughter except for the same cool grey eyes, seemed to take in Frank for the first time. Her lips tightened and she said:

"Are you the guy from Chicago? The one that's been visiting the Project?"

Frank admitted that he was, and had been.

Helen Renfield glared at him. He was taken aback, alarmed even, by the animosity in her eyes. It appeared out of nowhere and the full blast of it was aimed directly and unflinchingly at him across the table.

She said bitingly, "Checking up on your experiments? Seeing how far the sickness has spread, is that it?"

"What sickness do you mean?" Frank asked her quietly.

"No doubt you've some fancy scientific name for it. And something just as neat to explain it all away."

"Helen," Cal Renfield said placatingly, getting up and holding her arm. "Frank is a journalist, a writer, he's got nothing to do with the Project. He's on an assignment for his magazine, all right?" He raised his sparse eyebrows in Frank's direction and shook his head as if in apology.

"Does she mean the babies?"

"That's right," Helen Renfield said. "I see you know all about them." Her nostrils were pinched and white, the flesh below her cheekbones pulled taut. Her face was quite pale now and made to appear even more so in contrast with her hair.

"Frank didn't know a thing about them till I told him," Cal Renfield said, becoming annoyed himself. "Don't jump to conclusions without proof."

"I think that's good advice," Frank said, rising to his feet. He looked at Cal Renfield. "I don't think any of us should do that."

56

Helen turned to her father. She was almost a head taller. "You let him wriggle out of it, is that right? Did you tell him that this only started after they took over the Telluride Mine?" She glanced at Frank with narrowed eyes. "I suppose you'd call that coincidence, just like the storms we've been having."

One of the farmhands had risen and was standing at Frank's shoulder. He was lean and stringy, veins protruding on his arms, and Frank could smell dried sweat on him.

The man said, "Christ, fella, you'd better get the hell out of this town!"

Another of the men said, "Take it easy, John. Maybe he's got nothing—"

"I've got a kid at the hospital in Radium bin affected by your damn Project and whatever your scientist friends are doing out there. An eight-month-old baby girl lying there like a zombie." He clenched his lean red fists and raised them in a gesture of impotent fury. His eyes were hard and dry.

Frank felt sorry for the man but didn't see what he could do or how he ought to respond; it wasn't his fault, nor his responsibility.

Helen Renfield pulled at her father's arm, urging him to leave, and at that precise moment a low rumble of thunder echoed faintly in the distance, the onset of a storm rolling toward them from the Mount of the Holy Cross.

CHAPTER FIVE

Had Frank Kersh doubted or disbelieved Cal Renfield's account of the freak weather conditions along the Roaring Fork Valley (which in fact he hadn't) the storm that night would have swept his doubt aside and made him a firm believer.

It was spectacular, fearsome to behold, and torrential.

The blackness outside was total: a combination of low dark cloud, sweeping gusts of rain, and the night itself closing in around them until even the street lights were obscured in a dense pall of wind and water which buffeted the window of his room so that he thought it was going to shatter under the strain. Now and then a flicker of forked lightning licked across the mountain top, the dark streaming granite face standing out in stark relief, and then the blackness descended once more accompanied by a crash which jarred the light bulbs in their sockets and made the window frames creak.

It was the most vicious storm he had ever experienced and it was little comfort to know that it was probably due to the high altitude of the terrain:

instead of being above them the storm was actually around them, at ground level. If what Cal Renfield said was true about the frequency of the storms they had suffered over the past eighteen months it pointed to some severe disturbance in the lower stratosphere which the high rugged backbone of the Rockies had exacerbated and brought down upon itself. But of course there had to be a quite rational meteorological/geophysical explanation; the notion that it was some-how connected with—or even caused by—the Deep Hole Project was nonsense, the superstitious belief of ignorant people.

It was impossible to sleep, the noise and general psychological discomfort too great to allow prolonged relaxation, so Frank lay on the bed reading *Moby Dick*, a book he always carried with him in the hope of one day actually finishing it. It seemed the more he read the longer it got. He could have done with a drink but he didn't feel like disturbing his friendly hotel manager, Mr. Stringer.

He had just finished Ishmael's account of the habits of the Sperm Whale and was about to start Chapter 82, "The Honor and Glory of Whaling," when the bedside lamp dimmed and went out. A glance into the corridor told him that the power had failed and there wasn't a light showing anywhere. He looked at the luminous dial of his watch and saw that it was twelve-nineteen, which meant that the storm had been raging for more than an hour.

There was nothing else to do but lie in the pitch blackness listening to the sound of his own heartbeat and feeling the close tepid air pressing against his face and neck. His one fear was that the road to the east had been washed out and he would be delayed on his return trip: he had planned an early start, getting to Denver by mid-morning and taking Route 80 through Omaha, Des Moines, Davenport, and arriving in Chicago sometime during late evening. It was a fair drive but there shouldn't be any problem—providing the road between here and Denver was intact.

He was anxious to get back for a number of reasons. Apart from the fact that Perry Tolchard was expecting him and his desk would most likely be piled high with rewrites, he wanted to talk to somebody at the NIH, which had an office in Chicago. If there was anything at all—anything worth substantiating—in Cal Renfield's story about the babies born locally and their lack of normal development, then somebody at the National Institute of Health should have the facts and figures and quite probably an expert medical opinion on the cause. Almost certainly, Frank reasoned, it would have something to do with a virus infection or hereditary disease—meningitis or hydrocephalus—that a small percentage of infants were known to suffer from in the first months of life. But an incidence of one in three was unusually high and it wasn't surprising that the local community was disturbed and liable to lay the blame on whatever seemed strange or inexplicable, especially if it could be given the sinister label, "scientific research."

He lay in the warm darkness and listened to the storm slowly dying away. The lightning flashes became fainter and less frequent, the low grumbling roll of thunder moving northward over the town, and the fierce downpour slackened to a steady patter of rain which occasionally rattled against the window as if someone were throwing handfuls of rice against the glass.

It was this which finally lulled him to sleep, sliding into a shallow uneasy calm in which the sound of the rain became a shower of neutrinos slicing through the mountain and smashing into the detection tanks at the speed of light. And in the manner of dreams everything became confused so that it was the hotel manager, Stringer, who was in charge of the operation, wearing a white coat, Stetson and spurs; and Dr. Leach and Cal Renfield were interchangeable, a composite figure embodying the characteristics and mannerisms of both. Helen Renfield was there too, but she became transposed into the girl he had met out on the West Coast—this hybrid female diving from the gantry and swimming in a tank of perchloroethylene as if it were a sparkling blue sunlit pool up on Bel Air . . .

The morning light was raw, the air clear, and the temperature had dropped by at least four degrees. The storm had swept the sluggish humid layer out of the valley and there was a perceptible chill as the colder mountain air tumbled down from the peaks.

As he was coming out of the bathroom Frank met Spencer Tutt on the landing; he was carrying a pile of sheets, blankets and towels. The young man nodded a greeting and said in his lazy drawl, "We got the power back on, so you'll be able to eat breakfast. That were a daddy, weren't it?"

Frank agreed that it had been quite a storm. He said, "You get them pretty often, I believe."

"That we do. An' they're gettin' to be worse, I can tell you. The one last night was the worst yet." He

regarded Frank for a moment, his eyes set close together above the prominent sunburned beak of his
nose. "Looks like them scine-tists over at the Project
reaped what they sowed. An' it seems like nobody's
gonna lift a finger."

"What do you mean?"

"The old Telluride working was flooded last night.
Three or four men still down there, trapped by the
floodwater. They put out a call for volunteers but
there ain't nobody exactly rushin' to help." He
shrugged slightly, the wide rake of his bony shoulders
stretching the material of his shirt. He turned away.

"Isn't there a rescue team in the area?"

"Oh yeah," said Spencer Tutt over his shoulder.
"And we're it."

"Do you mean nobody's willing to help them?"
Frank said.

He found it hard to believe that the townspeople
could be so filled with the desire for revenge that it
overcame everything else. But it seemed he had seriously underestimated the depth of bitterness and
ill-feeling.

He said, "Is the road to the Project still open?"

"Far as I know. Bin no reports that the bridge is
down, anyways."

Frank stared after the young man's lean angular
back; he was shocked and momentarily at a loss. His
first positive thought was to wonder if the engineers
on the Deep Hole Project had the facilities to mount
a rescue operation . . . it was logical to assume they
would in case just such an emergency as this arose.
But had they been trained in underground search and
rescue? What was required was a team of men with

62

specialized training and knowledge who knew the local strata and were experienced in locating miners buried under rockfalls or cut off by underground streams. In the absence of such expert help the chances of reaching the trapped scientists were negligible.

It took almost an hour to get to the Project: the road above the bridge spanning Eagle River had been washed away in places and there had already been some attempts made at clearing the rubble and making the road passable. Tire tracks indicated that a number of vehicles had passed to and fro and Frank wondered if the scientists had been able to summon outside help.

But when he arrived it soon became evident that they hadn't. Professor Friedmann might have been a first-rate theorist in the field of neutrino astronomy but his grasp of practical matters—particularly when it came to organizing an underground rescue operation—was far too tentative and unsure, lacking the knowledge and ability to deploy men in the most effective manner.

There were two or three small groups standing around the compound, rather lost and aimless it seemed, and Professor Friedmann was talking with the senior engineer, a burly man wearing a bright yellow safety-helmet, the two of them standing at a trestle-table spread with maps and charts. Dr. Leach wasn't to be seen, Frank noted, and he wondered if he was one of the men trapped underground.

Professor Friedmann had a look in his eyes that could only be described as controlled panic. He nodded brusquely as Frank came up, tapping a ruler on the table in a rapid nervous tattoo, not really listening as the senior engineer explained the layout of the ventilation and water-drainage systems in the vicinity of the detection chamber. After a moment he interrupted the man and said, almost fervidly:

"Are they organizing a rescue team? Are they on their way?"

"No on both counts," Frank said. "And they don't intend to either."

"They have plenty of air," the senior engineer said, continuing his technical resume of the installation. "As far as we can tell the system is still functioning. If they managed to stay on the gantry above the water level then there's better than a fifty-fifty chance that they're okay. The drainage tunnels were only checked a couple of weeks ago and they were in good working order, so by now the level should be falling. I estimate—" he looked at his watch and calculated silently "—that within ten hours, fifteen at the outside, the chamber should be clear."

"Aren't you in telephone contact with them?" Frank asked.

Professor Friedmann shook his head. He looked grey and ill. "The line's dead," he said in a quiet voice. "We lost contact at midnight."

"How many men are down there?"

"Four. They went on duty at ten o'clock, just before the storm began. I was about to recall them—" his voice faltered "—but couldn't get through."

Frank moved up to the table and studied an elevation diagram of the detection chamber; it took him a moment to get his bearings, and when he had he said to the engineer, "Are these the ventilation shafts?"

The senior engineer looked at Professor Friedmann as if making sure that it was all right to speak, then he nodded. "There are three in the roof, two for inflow, one for extraction. We can't be a hundred per cent certain but we think they're still operational."

"How big are they?"

The senior engineer raised one grizzled eyebrow and shook his head. "I know what you're thinking and the answer is no: they're too small. And if they weren't too small it wouldn't do those four guys much good—those shafts are seamless aluminum, there's not a handhold anywhere. You can forget that."

"This is the main tunnel leading from the shaft—is that right?"

"Yeah, that's the one." The senior engineer's voice had quickened in response to Frank's queries, as if at last there was someone prepared to take an interest in the problem and make a constructive suggestion. He was a broad thick-set man with the kind of hands and wrists that can twist steel bars. He looked too as if he had been in the wars: there was an old deep scar across his forehead and the tip of his right index finger was missing.

"Have you been down to check the height of the water? Perhaps the tunnel isn't completely flooded. It's possible."

"There's no need to go down. There are sensors in the main shaft and we know from them that the lower level is flooded to the roof. There's just no way to get through until the water starts to drain off."

Frank said, "The lower level? You mean there's

more than one level in that area of the mine?"

"Sure, the place is a regular warren of them." The senior engineer pulled another chart forward and traced a blunt finger along a series of interconnecting tunnels. "The workings extend in every direction, some of them beyond the detection chamber—"

"Which is how far from the main shaft?"

"A helluva long way," the senior engineer said dourly. "Mile and a half, maybe more." He looked into Frank's eyes. "You're thinking of trying to reach the chamber by another route?"

"You're the engineer, you tell me. If we went down as far as this level and worked our way along we'd be within striking distance of the chamber. But it would all depend on there being an access point to the lower level; there isn't one marked on the diagram but that doesn't mean there isn't a natural fissure leading down to it. Do you recall having seen one?"

The senior engineer scratched his chin while he thought about it. He looked doubtful. "We did a lot of blasting in that area when we were constructing the chamber, opened up a few cracks here and there, but I don't remember breaking through to the lower level."

"Perhaps there's no real cause for alarm," Professor Friedmann said hopefully. His eyes were vague and frightened behind the blue-tinted spectacles. "They could very well be safe on the gantry, it's thirty feet high."

His voice betrayed the bland reassurance of what he was saying; it reminded Frank of a schoolboy telling a rather unconvincing fib that he doesn't expect anyone to believe.

"There are four men underground," the senior engineer said, spacing the words deliberately. "If that isn't cause for alarm, what the hell is?" He spread his hands on the table and stared down at the diagram as if by sheer concentration he could make the fissure appear, its position magically marked.

Frank said, "There's nothing to be lost by checking it out. If we get there and find there's no access point, we come back. But maybe in a mine as old as this there's a reasonable chance we could get through. Wouldn't you say so?" The question was addressed to the senior engineer. There didn't seem much point in soliciting Professor Friedmann's opinion.

"We need somebody with experience."

"I've been underground before now."

"A mile deep?"

"No," Frank said.

"I guess we can't be choosy. What would you say— a team of four?"

"Five plus a doctor."

Professor Friedmann seemed to wake out of a trance. "There's no doctor here. We have a medical orderly, will he do?"

"As the man said, this is no time to be choosy." Frank straightened up and looked at his watch. "I reckon it should take us two to three hours to get down and along the tunnel to within reasonable proximity of the chamber. Is there anyone who's familiar with the workings and can estimate our position underground with a fair degree of accuracy?"

"I've got two men who know that area pretty well."

"I'll take them both."

"And me."

"If you insist on coming but I think you should stay on the surface. We can relay any messages via a land-line and you can keep us informed on the weather situation. I wouldn't like to be caught down there during another freak thunderstorm."

The senior engineer nodded briskly. "All right, that sounds sensible to me. I'm Lee Merriam by the way."

"Frank Kersh."

"Okay, Frank, I'll have one of my men get the equipment together. Thank God that's one thing we're not short of." He turned to go.

"If there's a member of the scientific staff called Fawbert who'd like to come along, tell him he's welcome," Frank said.

Lee Merriam glanced back at Professor Friedmann, who said stonily, "That won't be possible; Fawbert is one of the men underground."

CHAPTER SIX

He half-expected to see bones gleaming in the beams of the lamps—the remains of prospectors long-dead calcified in the final rite of clawing at the rock face, their fleshless fingers clutching emptily at the dank musty air.

There were no human remains but there was other evidence that men had been scrabbling here in the darkness, seeking the elusive yellow grains which speckled the rock in the wild dream that tonight they would go to their beds rich men. Warped and rusting tracks, splintered and rotting beams, buckled iron trollies—the detritus of greed and abandoned hope littered the tunnels like carefully-preserved historical exhibits in a museum. The mine had yielded up its treasure and then been left to molder in dripping, creaking silence; and very slowly, with the infinite patience of nature, the earth was reclaiming its own, the vast pressure of billions of tons of rock squeezing tighter and healing the wounds so that in time nothing would remain but a tracery of scars.

The first stage had been easy. They had been lowered in the cage to one of the upper levels and entered a gallery which Lee Merriam had calculated was along the same line as that of the detection chamber. They were headed in the right direction but still separated from the lower level by 150 feet of what could well be solid rock. The plan of the mine gave no indication of natural faults or old shafts—nor indeed if it was possible to work their way along without progress being halted by a blocked tunnel. It was a blind gamble with no guarantee of success.

One of the engineers led the way, with Frank close behind and the others following on. They carried heavy-duty lamps, nylon ropes, a light-weight folding aluminum ladder and a small kit of basic medical supplies. Lee Merriam had suggested they take along wet-suits and breathing apparatus but Frank had vetoed the idea, saying that if they came to water too deep to wade through they wouldn't proceed any further: none of them had experience in negotiating underground water courses and it would be risking lives needlessly even to make the attempt. Fortunately the tunnel was mainly dry with here and there only a small stagnant pool formed by condensation. The one thing they all noticed was the smell: it was, as somebody remarked, "as if the mountain had halitosis." The air was chill and yet had a sour bad taste that Frank imagined to be coming from a large prehistoric animal decomposing in the darkness.

Not for the first time it occurred to him how susceptible the human mind was—in certain situations—to the suggestion that unknown terrors and supernatural forces lurked in the most innocuous of inanimate objects. The night before, sitting in the Cascade Hotel with Cal Renfield, he hadn't thought anything of the tales that the Telluride Mine was a haunted place; it had been nothing more or less than a bit of quaint local folklore that he had patiently listened to and then dismissed. That had been with a drink in front of him and in the comfortable environment of a well-lit room. Now the same story took on meaning, became real, changed from being a childish fairytale into something that just might have a basis in fact. The difference of course was that he had exchanged the bright outer world for this dank subterranean granite tomb which was the natural abode of spirits, phantoms and things that went bump in the night.

It was foolish imagination, he told himself, and for a rational man of the twentieth century rather weak and pathetic . . . yet he couldn't dismiss the notions lurking in his mind, nor dispel the sense of foreboding which seemed to squat like a heavy leaden lump in his chest.

The engineer at the head of the party—a man called Craig—halted every now and then to check his plan of the workings. They had left the main gallery some way back and were following one of the narrower side tunnels which intersected with other tunnels of varying sizes. At first Frank had tried to memorize the party's route, holding a plan of it in his head, but he soon lost track of the number of tunnels they entered, whether they had turned left or right, how far they had walked before turning into yet another tunnel—identical to the last one which was identical to the one before that and the one before that. It was hopeless. Everything depended on Craig knowing where he was going and, even more importantly, being absolutely sure of how to get back.

They had been following the labyrinth of tunnels for just over an hour when the engineer halted and called them forward. They clustered around him, the concentration of bright light reflecting the circle of faces which were already streaked with dust and shiny with perspiration. It was odd, Frank thought, that they should be sweating when the air was so chill; even the walls were exuding moisture.

Craig pointed to a cross marked on the plan. "As near as I can tell this is where we are now. It's directly above the detection chamber—that's if Lee got his calculations right and the map of these old workings is accurate to within fifty feet." He looked at Frank, his face set and serious. "Now where do we go from here?"

Frank studied the plan. "We investigate all the tunnels within this general area—" he traced a circle "—and see if we can find a shaft or a fissure leading downward. One of us—it had better be you, Craig—will remain here as our central reference point. The rest of us will take one hundred paces in each direction and check out the workings. One hundred paces, okay? Then we return to this spot and report. If we've found nothing we extend the circle by another hundred paces. If you come across something that looks interesting report back immediately. Don't investigate it yourselves, that's the one sure way to get into trouble. Report back here and we'll go in one party and check it out. If you lose your bearings stay exactly where you are and call out. *Don't move an inch.* Stay right there and call out and keep calling out and using your lamp as a beacon. Has everyone got that?"

The medical orderly had got it but he still wasn't happy. He had thin features and apprehensive eyes and a nervous habit of continually licking his lips. He cleared his throat and said, "Could I stay right here? I mean, I really don't think I could go out there on my own." He moistened his lips and smiled apologetically. "I'm sorry but I really couldn't."

"All right, you stay here with Craig."

Frank swept his lamp in an arc. The tunnel was pitted with workings, some of them no bigger than holes in the rock face, and ahead of them the tunnel divided, the smaller entrance partially blocked by rubble and collapsed beams. He shared the medical orderly's apprehension but they had come this far and there was no turning back. The four of them set off, Frank choosing to explore the offshoot of the main tunnel, clambering carefully through the triangle of rotten timbers and treating them like delicate porcelain; he had the uncomfortable feeling that if he breathed a shade too heavily the entire makeshift supporting structure would collapse with him underneath it.

He counted his paces. Providing the way ahead was straight, without side turnings, he shouldn't have any difficulty in finding his way back. This smaller tunnel was no wider than the outstretched span of his arms and he had to stoop slightly to avoid knocking his helmet against the roof. The floor was thick with dust and he was glad to see his progress plainly marked by a series of trailing footsteps.

After thirty paces the tunnel began to narrow and deviate to the right. It also seemed to be on a gradual slope, though it was difficult to be absolutely sure, his sense of orientation confined to this cramped dark space with no external point of reference.

Soon he was having to walk in a semi-crouch, which was punishing to his thigh muscles. But he consoled himself with the fact that—so far, at any rate—he hadn't had to make any abrupt turns or been faced with a choice of direction, which was what he feared most. As long as we keep on the straight and narrow, he told himself with a certain grim satisfaction, it should be child's play getting back. The tunnel was like a long curving tube and it reminded him of an intestine in the body of a large animal, himself a microbe burrowing into the dark interior, a rogue cancer cell seeking out a vital organ.

At seventy-five paces the tunnel became much narrower, so that he had to turn sideways and edge his way forward. It occurred to him that this might be the beginning of a natural fault because it was plainly too small to allow the passage of ore; the only other possibility was that it had been constructed as a linking tunnel between workings, and this turned out to be the most likely explanation, for after ten shuffling paces it opened up into a sizeable area and in the light of the lamp Frank could see heaps of rubble and other debris and the pock-marked rock face where the miners had excavated.

Before stepping forward to examine the area Frank found a small piece of whitish stone and marked the place he had emerged from, aware that it would be only too easy to lose his bearings. He swept the beam of light along the walls and moved slowly forward, crouching down to peer into the holes, most of which were quite shallow, a dozen feet into the rock or less. At the far end of the small cavern there was a tunnel —fairly wide and high—and he shone the light along it, nearly dropping the lamp in the dust when he saw what he thought was an answering flash of light. He held the lamp steady and there in the distance, unmistakably, was a light.

He tried to call out but his throat was parched. He swallowed and tried again, his voice dead and muffled and sounding strangely alien in his ears. There was no answer. He swivelled the lamp from side to side and the light in the distance copied the movement, and it was then the realization came to him that what he was seeing was in fact a reflection—there was something shiny at the far end of the tunnel reflecting the beam back at him.

He was relieved and also curious. What kind of material could have retained such a bright surface finish after being underground for fifty, sixty years— maybe longer? Could it be a mirror? Or some form of metal that had withstood corrosion and oxidization? But that was plainly impossible, for such metals had been unknown when the mine was in use.

His hundred paces were up, and he knew he ought to make his way back, but the object at the end of the tunnel baffled and intrigued him. He thought: I'll check it out and then return. It's in direct line with the cavern so all I have to do is turn through 180 degrees and head straight back. There's nothing in the way; I can't go wrong if I keep to the main tunnel.

He held the lamp in front of him and watched its reflection advancing toward him, the bobbing beam of light moving eerily in the pitch blackness. It was further away than he had realized—a good deal further, in fact. He walked on, occasionally stumbling over rocks half-buried in the dust, feeling the cold sweat on the back of his neck and beginning to regret his decision to go beyond the hundred paces. He had given the others explicit instructions not to proceed one step further and already he was breaking his own strict rule.

The glare of the light dazzled him as he approached the object: it was black and smooth, he now saw, a flat highly-polished surface without a blemish. It blocked the tunnel completely, a sheer mirror-like wall of solid black rock.

This was no natural object. Nothing in nature was this smooth, unless it was glacier ice, and certainly no rock strata could adopt this formation without being cut, machined and polished by mechanical means. Had it been buried here for some purpose? Was it perhaps connected with the Project, part of the neutrino detection equipment?

Frank couldn't imagine what it might be, or what its function was, or how it had come to be here, nearly a mile underground beneath the Mount of the Holy Cross. For no discernible reason he thought of the Telluric Faith and how the Tellurians believed the mountain to be the focal point of some kind of supernatural power, a cosmic force-field where lines of energy intersected and formed an aura of Earth Power . . .

Where had that phrase come from? Cal Renfield hadn't used it, he was quite certain, and neither had the Tellurians during their Prayer Meeting. Frank closed his eyes and rested his forehead against the cool black rock. Something seemed to vibrate inside his head as if a million molecules were being jostled by a high-voltage current. Behind his eyelids a series of phosphorescent lights whirled in deepest space and he began to feel the ground trembling and falling away. He tried to hold on, to cling to the rock, but it was like trying to grab hold of an oiled glass surface. Was it an earth tremor far below or a rockfall blocking the tunnel? He opened his eyes and saw cracks appearing everywhere, jagged fissures advancing like dark sinister lightning flashes along the floor of the tunnel.

Everything was shaking and he became suddenly aware of a high-pitched oscillation which seemed to emanate from the vibrating rock. The sound was at the limit of human hearing, experienced through the skull and bones rather than actually heard, and it increased in intensity until it became physical pain, cutting like cheese-wire through the cerebral cortex and piercing the nervous system like needles of pure white light. Yet curiously the sensation was tolerable, as if the pain was more imagined than real, and Frank Kersh wondered if any of this was actually happening or was it all illusory, the spinning molecules inside his head creating this frenzy of noise and movement and disordered perception.

Then he was sliding, not fast but gently, the smooth black rock supporting him and carrying him down into the lower depths. The lamp was gone, he had lost it, he was adrift in a subterranean world of sliding blackness and panic rose up in his throat like nausea. He was descending into the earth, falling slowly as in a nightmare toward the bottomless black void at the core of the planet and there was nothing to save him, nothing to reach out and touch, not the faintest speck of light anywhere at all.

His feet were wet.

He had the distinct sensation that water had seeped into his boots and that he was standing ankle-deep in freezing cold water. This is a funny kind of hell, Frank thought, and moved his right foot experimentally. There was the swirling sound of water and he felt the drag of it impeding his movement. Tentatively he took a step forward, then another, holding his arms out in front of his face in case he walked into something. The water sucked at his boots but it was a reassuring sound and the fact of having wet feet didn't upset him in the least.

The ground was hard and firm, like concrete, and he gained confidence, making steady progress through the watery darkness. He could smell something pungent—perchloroethylene—and the thought of this preoccupied him until he walked into the side of a stainless steel tank. He was in the detection chamber.

The layout of the place was still clear in his mind—the four tanks in line down the center of the chamber and the gantry at one end—and he guessed right first time, choosing to follow his right hand, and eventually arrived at the metal stairway which he climbed thankfully and with immense gratitude to God, Providence, or whatever It was that moved the heavens.

After searching through the desk he found a flashlight, and a single sweep of the gantry was enough to reveal everything he needed to know and been afraid he might find. Four bodies lay sprawled about, their clothing wrinkled and damp, looking like rag dolls that had been tossed down by a child too weary to play any more. Fawbert was one of them, his long fair hair plastered across his eyes like pale seaweed.

There was nothing to be done, nothing that could be done which would make a jot of difference. Frank sat down and waited, propping the flashlight on the desk so that it shone into the chamber, away from the corpses.

Lee Merriam was the first to arrive. He led a party of men through the main tunnel and gave a shout of jubilation when he saw the light. He came splashing across the chamber and climbed the stairway, the smile lingering on his face for several incredulous moments when he saw who was seated at the desk. It was evident that he couldn't take it in; the fact had registered but remained incredible.

He said, "We thought you were dead."

Frank said, "So did I."

"Is there anyone else . . . ?"

Frank shielded his face from Lee Merriam's flashlight. "Over there." He nodded into the darkness. "The water level must have gone way above the gantry, almost to the roof."

Lee Merriam was still staring at Frank as if he might not really exist. "The rest of your party made it back to the surface, but after the tremor they reckoned you were—"

"Then there was an earth tremor, I didn't imagine it?"

"You sure didn't imagine that last one. Shook the entire mountain. They were waiting for you to come back when everything started shaking. The entrance to the tunnel you were in collapsed and they had to beat it out of there fast. Craig said that you wouldn't have stood a chance. There was nothing they could do, not a thing. How in hell did you get out? And how did you get down here?"

"How in hell is right." Frank stood up and looked down at his boots. "I got my feet wet and that's about all. You can take it from me, as a confirmed atheist of twenty years' standing I'm beginning to have serious doubts."

It was no answer at all but the only one he could give. He didn't believe in black, glasslike, vibrating rocks any more than Lee Merriam did: probably less, because he prided himself on being the calm, rational man of science. To explain it away by the convenient use of the supernatural would have been too easy—and he doubted whether he could live with the look of mocking skepticism that would surely have been Lee Merriam's first reaction. He knew that it would have been his.

It took an hour and twenty minutes to return to the surface with the four bodies. Frank was amazed that it was still daylight. He seemed to have been underground for a long time, certainly longer than the five hours that had actually elapsed. But it was only mid-afternoon and the world seemed remarkably clean and new after the foul-smelling tunnels a mile below, the dirt and dampness and moldering decay.

Yet even now the mysteries of the mountain still hadn't finished with them.

When the bodies of the four men were examined by the medical orderly he could find no trace of water in their lungs. He admitted quite openly that he wasn't a qualified doctor and therefore might be mistaken about what had, or hadn't, been the cause of death. But in his humble opinion they most certainly hadn't died from drowning.

CHAPTER SEVEN

Professor Edmund Friedmann smiled hesitantly and held out his long pale hands as if in a gesture of conciliation. His thin, rather austere face was a study in guarded amiability, rather like that of an uninvited guest at a party, unsure of his welcome. And yet, Frank Kersh reflected, it was he who was the "guest" —he was on Professor Friedmann's home territory.

Dr. Leach was also present, but he hardly acknowledged Frank's presence, sitting hunched in the chair, his large powerful hands clasped in front of him in the manner of someone waiting for a lecture to begin.

Professor Friedmann said, "You know Dr. Leach, of course."

"We met yesterday," Frank said. "Briefly."

"Remarkable," said Professor Friedmann, shaking his head in wonder. "When Craig and the others returned we really had given you up for dead. It's a miracle you survived."

"For once I wouldn't dispute the choice of that word. I still don't know what happened, but miraculous is as good an explanation as any." Frank lit a cigarette and sat back. He felt that he had the psychological advantage. There were secrets on both sides and he wasn't prepared to reveal his until Friedmann and Leach felt an obligation to confide in him.

"We're most grateful for your efforts," said Professor Friedmann. "As you'll have gathered we hadn't made adequate preparations for an underground rescue operation; to be honest with you, Kersh, the possibility of something like this happening had never occurred to us."

"There's always a risk involved when men are working underground. But I can understand that as a scientific research establishment the thought of some natural disaster was the last thing in your minds." He wondered whether he had sufficiently disguised the implied irony so as to make it a statement of fact rather than criticism.

Dr. Leach said in his low growling voice, "These things happen. I don't see how we can be held responsible for something entirely outside our control. But it means months of work wasted and the program held up while the equipment is repaired. And there's the question of cost: the Institute mightn't be prepared to invest another half million dollars to make good the damage."

"Or replace the men who died," Frank said.

"Technical staff are no problem," said Dr. Leach obliviously. "There are always more than enough post-graduates eager and willing to participate in advanced research projects of this kind."

"Even at the risk of losing their lives?"

Dr. Leach fixed Frank with his hard dark stare. "An unfortunate occurrence," he said stolidly.

"Random, unexpected, and one which could not have been foreseen."

"Not all that random according to the people of Gypsum. The editor of the local newspaper told me that freak thunderstorms were happening more often and with increasing intensity." Frank looked at Professor Friedmann, and added, "Over the past eighteen months, that is."

Professor Friedmann avoided his eyes and glanced for a second at his colleague. He picked up a pen from the desk and tapped out a rapid, uneasy rhythm, then needlessly adjusted his blue-tinted spectacles. He seemed to make up his mind about something and said abruptly, "We know very well what the local people think of the Project. We've had nothing but trouble from them ever since we arrived. They blame every calamity, every minor disturbance on the Deep Hole Project, as if our experiments could in any way affect the external world. They're ignorant and superstitious and out to cause trouble."

"And there isn't the slightest possibility that they could be right."

"Of course not, of course not," Professor Friedman said waspishly. "For heaven's sake, Kersh, you're a man with scientific training, you know enough about solar neutrino detection to realize that what we do here couldn't possibly interfere with atmospheric conditions. The experiments are carried out in a sealed self-contained environment beneath a mile of solid rock. It's nonsense to suggest that they might be the cause of these thunderstorms we've been having. Complete nonsense."

"At a detection rate of one neutrino per month

I'd be inclined to agree with you," Frank said. He looked from one to the other. "If that's actually the rate at which you've been detecting them."

"Has anyone said that it isn't?" asked Dr. Leach. He unclasped his powerful hands and turned his dark hooded gaze in Frank's direction. It was disconcerting to see the upper half of a fully-grown man gradually merging into a foreshortened trunk and stunted legs; the effect was somehow obscene, the evil demonic trickery of a fairground freak show.

"No, no one has," Frank admitted. "But secrecy tends to breed suspicion, and neither Professor Friedmann nor yourself were exactly willing to discuss your research data in any detail. It isn't classified material, and the technique is well known to other workers in the field, so the question naturally presented itself as to whether you were hiding certain information—"

"For what reason?" Professor Friedmann interrupted, his tone defensive and at the same time wary. It reminded Frank of a man treading cautiously through a minefield, anticipating an explosion any second.

"I don't know." He tried a shot in the dark. "Perhaps you've detected many more neutrino interactions than fit comfortably with current theories and you don't know yourselves what to make of them." He watched Professor Friedmann carefully. "Or if not an abundance of neutrinos, antineutrinos."

Dr. Leach had gasped—or was it merely the bored sigh of someone running short of patience? But he was near to something; the sense of it hung in the air like static electricity.

Professor Friedmann cleared his throat nervously. He said, "Your assumption is partly true. The findings show that—"

"We will not discuss our findings," Dr. Leach contradicted him flatly. "Kersh is a snooping journalist and we are in no way obliged to reveal *anything* of the work carried out on the Deep Hole Project. His only motive is to publish misleading and unsubstantiated reports concerning our activities and to draw conclusions for which he is unqualified and ill-equipped. I will not allow my work to be interrupted by interfering outsiders whose knowledge of neutrino astronomy is non-existent."

Professor Friedmann nodded, as if in agreement, but then surprised Frank by saying, "I take your point, Karl, and I sympathize with it, but at the same time we do have a wider obligation to the scientific community to publish our results, rather than holding onto them as if they were our own personal property. We are merely the custodians of the information, not its exclusive owners. It's our task to explore, to investigate, to detect and identify, to compile data— and then to divulge what we've discovered. Kersh is right in that sense, and he's also right in pressing us for information." He set his spectacles more firmly on his nose. "We need outside help, you've said so yourself. We need the help of experienced astrophysicists to interpret the results."

"But not now," Dr. Leach said with emphasis. "Not yet. We're not ready. The program has at least another year to run before we can even begin to think of consulting other people in the field. We agreed on a three-year program and we must keep to it. I refuse

86

to allow outside interference at this delicate and crucial stage."

"Even though the experiments might be having a detrimental effect on the local community," Frank said. "On the babies born during the past eighteen months, for instance."

"I've said, and I'll repeat it," responded Professor Friedmann heatedly. "There is no evidence to suggest that antineutrino events have the slightest effect on anything, animate or inanimate, outside the sub-nuclear region. The Earth itself produces vast quantities of antineutrinos every nano-second, they're passing through us this very instant, but because they don't interact with the atoms in our bodies there is absolutely zero effect. Look at the literature, Kersh, and you'll see. The phenomena is thoroughly documented and proven beyond all doubt."

After a moment Frank said, "Is the level of antineutrinos from the Sun much greater than expected?"

"Yes," Professor Friedmann said shortly. He looked at Dr. Leach and held his gaze. "By a factor of two hundred."

"That's quite a jump. How do you account for it?"

"At the moment we can't." Professor Friedmann seemed perturbed about something. His eyes passed over the computer printout on the desk; he pressed his pale slender hands together and met Frank's look squarely. "You might as well know the rest of it, Kersh. The antineutrinos we've detected and identified aren't coming from the Sun. We've tried to pinpoint the source and it seems that the bulk of them are emanating from a region which corresponds to Sagittarius A, which is directly in the galactic center of the Milky Way. We don't know why there should be an increased emission of anti-particles from the heart of the Galaxy but all our studies indicate that the Earth is receiving antineutrinos from a central region of less than 0.02 arc seconds in size. Whatever it is that's transmitting them must be the most powerful source of radiation in our Galaxy. Beyond that we enter into the realm of theory and speculation."

"And what's your theory, Dr. Leach?" Frank asked the dark intense man sitting in the chair opposite.

"I haven't formulated a theory. I'm not a theoretical physicist; my function is to detect and identify neutrinos and their antiparticle equivalents reaching the earth from deep space."

"Which is precisely why we need to consult with other scientists whose job it is to interpret our results," Professor Friedmann told him, continuing the argument. "We already have enough data for them to work from, and now that the program is temporarily suspended we should use it as an opportunity to elicit outside help."

Dr. Leach shook his head, a stubborn child defying reason, logic and common sense. He would not be swayed. "When the time is *right*. The time is not yet right. We need at the very least another full year's results before we are in a position to present conclusive evidence. I will not be rushed into this, not after two years' solid work. I will see it through."

Frank said, "The people of Gypsum might have other ideas."

Dr. Leach smiled, a patronizing twist of the lips. "The people of Gypsum interest me less than particles moving at the speed of light, Mr. Kersh. And for someone with a supposedly scientific background you seem to be more in sympathy with them than the Project. You're not taken in by their childish superstitions and penny-ante religious cults, are you?"

"I don't know if 'taken in' is the right way to describe it, Dr. Leach. You'd have to be deaf, dumb and blind not to know that something very strange is happening along the Roaring Fork Valley. Maybe it has nothing to do with the Project; yesterday I was inclined to believe that, but now I'm not at all sure. If what I've been told is true—about the babies born locally, for one thing—then somebody ought to investigate and find out what the hell's going on. And don't underestimate the mood of the people down there. Feelings are running high at the moment—about as high as your antineutrino count."

Professor Friedmann said anxiously, "We've been quite open with you, Kersh, and in return I'd like your assurance that everything we've told you will remain strictly confidential—at least till Dr. Leach and myself have reviewed the situation and decided how we plan to proceed. If we decide to release the information I see no reason why we can't do it through *Science Now*, but I need to have your word that none of this will go any further until you hear from me again. I think that's fair and equitable. Do you agree?"

Frank nodded. "Yes I think it is, Professor. But what if you decide not to release the information? Would you still expect me to say nothing? Keep it under wraps?"

"We'll think about that if and when the situation arises."

"Pretty much in the same way that you thought

about rescuing the four men trapped underground," Frank said, this time the irony undisguised.

"It's a sad loss, I agree," said Professor Friedmann with what appeared to be genuine feeling. "If I could have done anything at all to save them from drowning I wouldn't have hesitated for one second."

"I believe you," Frank said, standing up. "Only you're forgetting that drowning is the one thing they didn't die from."

Part Two

THE PROPHESY

CHAPTER ONE

Frank stood at the high counter and thought what he wanted to say, and more importantly, how it should be expressed. The cable had to be couched in terms of a routine inquiry so as not to arouse undue curiosity and yet it was vital that Fred Lockyer clearly understood the need for an urgent, immediate response. Perhaps if he included a small joke; no, that wouldn't be right. The message had to be serious and to the point without giving anything away.

He didn't feel that he was breaking his word. Professor Friedmann had asked him not to reveal anything of the research carried out at the Deep Hole Project and he was keeping faithfully to the agreement: he was simply asking for up-to-date information on neutrinos and antineutrinos and the latest findings of physicists investigating that range of subnuclear particles known as hadrons—those which strongly interacted with other particles within the atomic nucleus. Fred Lockyer wasn't himself actively engaged in such research, but as Lecturer in High Energy Physics at the University of Illinois he kept abreast of what was happening all over the world and would know, if anybody did, what were the latest theories and hypotheses put forward by the particle physicists.

The question was, would Frank's present location give the game away? Fred wouldn't have heard of Gypsum (at least it was most unlikely) but all he had to do was glance at a map of the area to realize that it was within spitting distance of the Solar Neutrino Research Station funded by the US Institute of Astrophysics. It was a risk Frank would have to take —and so, unwittingly, would Friedmann and Leach.

Eventually he composed the message, reasonably satisfied that he had got the tone just about right. The crucial factor was whether Fred Lockyer would reply quickly. He had tried to imply a degree of urgency instead of stating it openly by saying MOVING ON SOON STOP PREFERABLE YOU CABLE REPLY IF POSSIBLE CARE OF CASCADE HOTEL. That should do it, he hoped; Fred was an amenable sort of guy who would bust a gut for a friend.

He came out into warm, gentle sunshine and paused for a moment to survey the street. There was a quiet bustle of mid-morning activity as housewives did their shopping at the Self-Save Supermart and across at the bank a small group of businessmen stood on the sidewalk, chatting and slapping each other on the shoulder. A customer was testing a pair of binoculars in front of the Gypsum Camera Center store, and on the corner a couple of dogs were fornicating, oblivious to passing traffic.

It was a normal everyday scene, no different to what was happening in a thousand small towns all over America, and yet in a curious way it seemed unreal, almost dreamlike, for he couldn't rid his mind of the images of musty subterranean passages and the detection chamber with its stainless steel tanks and the four bloated bodies huddled on the gantry. He thought: This is another world, this bright sunny outdoors, so friendly and reassuringly familiar. These people are living on the skin of the planet, unaware of what lurks beneath them, like insects skating on the surface of a pond. The vast bulk of the Earth is hidden away, directly beneath their feet, extending downward for thousands of miles, but for them it doesn't exist because they never give it a moment's thought. This is their "real world" and they never suspect it's mere surface show, literally skin-deep, and that the actual living core of the planet is shut away from their sight, trillions of tons of it upon which a humanoid form of life is permitted to crawl.

And what would they say if he told them that thousands of neutrinos and antineutrinos were passing through their bodies at this instant of time? Equally unreal, of course, because they couldn't see or feel them. This was the *real* world (they could see it and feel it) and anything that didn't affect them might just as well not exist. But the interesting question—which Frank Kersh would have liked to have put to them—was on what basis does one judge reality? The thin envelope of the biosphere was one limited and severely restricted slice of reality; the inner hidden core of the planet was another, much greater one; and the invisible neutrinos and antineutrinos moving at the speed of light were a form of reality which pervaded all space—every single cubic centimeter of space throughout the Universe. So what, in reality, constituted the real?

These people living out their tiny lives inhabited a stratum of space-time which was so incredibly insignificant as to be almost ethereal. Had they been granted an extension to their feeble and severely-restricted range of sensory perceptions they might have gained an inkling of what lay beyond this narrow plane of existence which they called reality. And not only beyond them in the sense of being "out there," but all around them, occupying the same space and time ... the waves of cosmic radiation washing over them from space, the subnuclear particles passing through their "real world" as if it were a patch of mist, the entire array of microwaves, infra-red rays, x-rays, ultra-violet rays, gamma rays, particles and antiparticles for which this sunny street with its people, stores, cars and copulating dogs had less basis in reality than a momentary passing dream and no more substance than images projected onto a blank wall.

It was a truism that people couldn't stand too much reality, but in truth they experienced hardly any reality at all. They possessed a smaller range of perception of the Universe around them than did a blind burrowing mole of its dark earthy environment. They looked out at the world with blind eyes, listened to its whisperings with deaf ears, and all along believed themselves to be the focal point of consciousness, the arbiter of intelligence, the only true and valid constant against which to measure objective reality.

And what of himself? Frank thought wryly. Perhaps he was blind too, in a different sense. He glanced around him, suddenly apprehensive, feeling he was being observed. There was no one watching, his instincts had deceived him. Then it hit him: he raised his eyes above the rooftops and there was the presence of the mountain, remarkably near in the clear morning light, the flimsiest wisp of cloud, like a brushstroke, obscuring the peak. The Tellurians believed the Mount of the Holy Cross to possess some kind of dynamic force. He had scoffed at their beliefs but now he understood how continually living in its shadow could evoke such strange and powerful emotions. The rational man of science, he mocked himself. He was no better than the people in the street; at least their ignorance excused them, but being aware of his own ignorance should have made him a wiser person. He doubted that it did.

The office of the *Roaring Fork Bulletin* was further along the main street, indistinguishable from the store-fronts either side—a gunsmith's and a dry-cleaner's—except for the absence of a window display and instead the front page of last week's issue taped inside a glass-fronted frame: *Recreation Resort for Great Eagle Dam? Lightning Kills Dotsero Farmworker. Rifle Wins Rio Blanco County League.*

Still wearing the creased white cotton suit, which Frank reckoned must be the newspaper editor's badge of office in these parts, Cal Renfield was seated at a large oval desk contemplating a rough page layout, some of which was already blocked in with half-tones and criss-crossed areas indicating copy. A mug of black coffee cooled at his elbow.

He levered himself into a semi-standing position, and when they had shaken hands flopped down again, his belly reverberating with the shock wave.

"My staff have taken the day off," Cal Renfield said, gesturing at the empty office with a hand that reminded Frank of a small pink pin cushion.

"You have staff?" Frank said good naturedly.

"Sure I have staff. All one of them. Do you want some coffee?"

"No thanks," Frank said, and then changed his mind.

Cal Renfield nodded toward the electric coffee pot and invited him to help himself. As Frank was doing this the small balding man said, "Don't you slick city reporters ever wear suits? All I've ever seen you in is denims, polo-neck sweaters and wind-cheaters. Is that the new hip style for Chicago news-papermen?"

Frank did a mannequin's twirl. "Today's ensemble is leather," he intoned in the arch portentous tones of the fashion commentator. "Note the neat little colored leather side-panels sewn into the body of the garment, *so* useful for carrying all the essentials of the writer's trade: pens, pencils, notebooks, erasers, portable typewriters."

"From what I heard, a safety-helmet, pick-axe and a pair of miner's boots would be a darn sight more useful." Cal Renfield offered a pack of cigarettes, his grey eyes shrewd and watchful.

"So you heard about that?" Frank said. He took a cigarette and lit them both. His hand was perfectly steady.

"I'm the local newshound," Cal Renfield reminded him. "They wouldn't allow me to visit the Project but I spoke with Lee Merriam, who's a regular guy, and

97

and he gave me the salient facts. As we newshounds say." His soft round features sobered and his eyes became flat, without expression. "It didn't help the men trapped below ground much."

Frank drank his coffee.

"What happened exactly?"

"I thought you said Lee Merriam told you."

"He did. Some of it."

"The salient facts."

"Lee wasn't underground when the tremor started. You were."

"We were underground," Frank said. "There was an earth tremor. End of story."

Cal Renfield nodded his head slowly. He sniffed. "For a reporter your power of recall isn't what I'd call shit-hot."

"I keep telling you, Cal, I'm not a reporter—I'm a feature writer with a science magazine. What happened is probably what Lee Merriam told you. I don't want to bore the ass off of you by repeating it."

"But you found the bodies?"

"Yes. They were on the gantry."

"What gantry is that?"

"You've never been down to the detection chamber?"

Cal Renfield smiled. "Do you think they'd allow the editor of the local newspaper to look at that vital top secret installation of theirs? No way, brother. No chance."

"Who told you it was top secret?"

"Friedmann. When they moved in I went up to interview him and he gave me a long rigmarole about top secret this and classified that. I got the impression they were engaged on some kind of advanced research for the government. Isn't that so?"

"In a way it is," Frank said, reminding himself that caution was the watchword of the day. "They're funded by a government agency, the Institute of Astrophysics. But I'd hardly describe the work they do as top secret."

"Okay," said Cal Renfield, blowing a plume of smoke at the ceiling. "You found the bodies on the gantry. Which is in the detection chamber, and—"

"There isn't a lot to say about dead bodies."

"Presumably they were drowned."

"They were found at the bottom of a flooded mine," Frank said, sticking to the literal truth.

"Did the tremor have anything to do with it?"

"In what way?" Frank asked, sipping his coffee and squinting at a large blown-up photograph of what looked like a steel smelting plant. He turned it over and read the typed caption: *US Bureau of Mines Shale Oil Plant, Grand Valley, Col.*

Cal Renfield sighed. "You're not the easiest of people to extract information from, you know that? I want the background stuff, not the official version. Was there anything at all that struck you as being out of the ordinary? Hell, Frank, you were first on the scene, practically an eye-witness."

"I've told you, they were already dead when I got there. The chamber had been flooded by the storm and there was no way of reaching them until the water subsided. Didn't Lee Merriam tell you all this?"

"Yeah." Cal Renfield drank the last of his coffee and studied the half-completed layout in front of him. "I just got the feeling there was more to it than that." He glanced up at Frank with his shrewd grey eyes. "You know, my newshound's sixth sense."

Frank moved around the office looking at the files of cuttings and news agency reports. He was on Cal Renfield's side: he was sympathetic to the man and wanted to help him but at the same time it would have been a mistake—and a betrayal of confidence—to have revealed anything of what he had learned about the Project's research program. And it was unlikely that the editor would have grasped the significance of a concentrated emission of antineutrinos reaching them from the center of the Galaxy. For the moment Frank had to play it cool, giving the appearance of an interested if slightly perplexed bystander.

He approached the desk where Cal Renfield was working, saying casually, "You mentioned the other evening that some kids had been born around here who exhibited strange behavior patterns. Where are they, local hospital?"

"We don't have a hospital in Gypsum. They're over in Radium receiving intensive care. Why do you ask?"

"I'd like to see them if possible. How far is Radium?"

"About fifteen miles north of here, the other side of Mount Powell." Cal Renfield pursed his lips together, like a small pink button. "What's your interest in them, Frank? Changing your views?"

"I'm interested in anything that bears investigation. How do I go about arranging a visit?"

"I could do that for you," Cal Renfield said after a moment's thought. "I know one of the doctors in the hospital, Bob Bragg. Used to have a practice in

Gypsum for a couple of years, then got taken on as a staff medico. Do you want me to fix it for you?"

"If possible, Cal. I'd appreciate it."

"See what I can do," Cal Renfield said, reaching for the phone. He was about to dial when Helen Renfield came in from the street, struggling with a large bulky photographer's case and a tripod. She dumped the equipment in a corner and straightened up, pressing her hands into the small of her back.

"You know my staff," Cal Renfield said to Frank, and then to Helen, "Did you get it?"

"I got it," she said briefly, looking at Frank's left shoulder but not his face. "I hate to tell you this, but taking pictures of a calf with five legs is not my idea of investigative journalism. It's hardly going to make the front cover of *Time*."

"Might make the front cover of *Stockbreeders Gazette*," Frank said jocularly.

Helen Renfield didn't think the witticism merited a response. She went to the coffeepot and poured herself a cup. Her red hair was drawn back from her face and tied in a schoolgirl bunch at the back. She wore very little make-up, just a touch of mascara to highlight her eyes, and with her checkered shirt and cowgirl jeans she might have been a college kid helping out with the Saturday morning chores. The paleness—almost austere tautness—in her face that Frank had noticed previously hadn't been a symptom of anger, apparently, for it was here now, complementing her large widely-spaced grey eyes which were ever alert for wooden nickels.

Frank wondered about her; she intrigued him; there was an inner cold calm and unequivocal certainty about her that he had seen in many young people, their principles uncompromised, their scruples still intact. They had seen the world, summed it up, sorted out the genuine from the fake—all without having achieved or accomplished anything. They had read the rule book but hadn't yet begun to play the game.

"I'm fixing it for Frank to visit the hospital in Radium," Cal Renfield said. He hadn't yet dialed the number.

His daughter looked up sharply. She looked at her father, not at Frank.

"Why?"

"I guess because he wants to see the babies," Cal Renfield said placidly.

"Is he a doctor?"

"Why not ask the man? That's him standing there."

"I'm not a doctor but I was trained in biochemistry. I do know something about human physiology."

"So you're going to astound the world of medical science and tell the doctors where they went wrong, is that it?"

Cal Renfield raised his eyebrows as if apologizing for a relative with bad table manners. He put the receiver down and propped his chin on his roly-poly fist.

Frank shook his head and smiled, pacing himself, not going to allow this young girl to rattle him or bamboozle him into an argument. He watched her for a moment and for the first time became aware of a tension between them that wasn't based on antagonism or positive dislike.

He said, "Any phenomena outside the norm interests me. There has to be a reason why these babies are behaving strangely—"

"Phenomena!" Helen said, glaring at him. "That's a swell two-dollar word to describe newborn babies that just lie there like vegetables. Wish I was a scientist, it must be great to wander through life looking for 'phenomena.' What do you call a car smash—a terminal automotive situation?"

"Whatever you might think, Miss Renfield, I'm in no way responsible for their condition. You seem to think the Project is in some way to blame, and you also believe that I have some connection with the Project. Both hypotheses, as we scientists say, are false. Not only that, they're founded on a total lack of evidence. As an investigative reporter you should know better than to make accusations which aren't substantiated by the facts. And what facts do you have? None."

"A good reporter relies on instinct too," Helen reminded him. "There's something going on up at the Telluride Mine, something that's not right. I don't know what it is, I don't have any 'facts,' but when people are tight-mouthed about something you can bet they've got a big fat juicy secret sitting there waiting to be found out."

"And what has that got to do with my wanting to visit the hospital in Radium?" Frank asked, not unreasonably he felt.

"You're on their side."

"Whose side?"

"The scientists on the Deep Hole Project."

Frank shrugged and appealed to Cal Renfield.

"What do I have to do to convince your daughter that I'm not Baron Frankenstein? Next time I'll bring my evil green potion and turn you all into toads. What do you want me to say?" he asked the girl. He threw up his hands and turned away. "Not that it really matters."

"All right," Helen said abruptly. "Say that we believe you."

"Your father believes me already."

Cal Renfield, in the act of lighting another cigarette, glanced keenly through the rising blue smoke, but didn't say anything.

"Say that we do," the girl continued. She folded her arms and faced him. "We're not scientists, we don't understand what the Project is for or what it's supposed to be doing—"

"It's quite simple," Frank interjected. "I've explained it to your father."

"He's explained it to me and it's not quite simple," Cal Renfield said, blowing volumes of smoke into the air. He propped his chin on his hand, watching them both.

"That's it exactly," Helen said. She looked at him intently. "We don't know the kind of questions to ask because we're not scientists. All right now, you've got a scientific background, you can ask the questions and spot if anything is wrong or doesn't seem to fit. You know what I mean?"

"Yes of course I do." Frank looked from daughter to father. "You want me to spy on them for you."

"It isn't spying, it's finding out the truth about what's happening in this valley," Helen said with some fervor. Her face was more animated now, her grey eyes sparkling with an intensity that surprised him. "That's if you're genuinely interested in finding out."

"Why not come with me to Radium and see how genuinely interested I am," Frank said. He was looking directly at her and her gaze faltered and dropped away. "What about it, Cal? Can you spare the time?"

"You mean you're offering me an excuse to get out of this goddamn office for a couple of hours?" Cal Renfield threw down the felt-tip marker and struggled to his feet, attempting to fasten his cotton jacket across the ponderous swell of his stomach. "Your car or mine?"

CHAPTER TWO

The town of Radium, as Cal Renfield had said, was only fifteen miles to the north, but it took them all of forty minutes to get there because the route was via Rabbit Ears Pass, which skirted the western slope of Mount Powell. On the way they passed through McCoy and Toponas—small townships along Blue River—and then took the right-hand fork to Radium, which lay between Kremmling and Troublesome. This area bordered on the White River Plateau, which was less a plateau than a series of foothills, like wrinkles in a blanket, riddled with small towns and villages: Steamboat Springs, Skull Creek, Maybell and Dinosaur to the west, and further north Hot Sulphur Springs, Coalmont and Lulu City.

Frank drove the Toronado carefully on the narrow twisting roads, taking in as much of the scenery as he could. It was magnificent country. This was the very heartland of the Rocky Mountains which straddled the Continental Divide like a heavy saddle-pack thrown over a mule's back. Sharp granite peaks faded into misty blueness in the distance, ranged up one behind the other as if waiting their turn in the

106

queue. In the valleys it was lush and green, and along Blue River the flashing white triangular sails of small sailing boats leaned together to take advantage of the breeze.

On the other side of Rabbit Ears Pass, following the meandering course of what appeared to be a dried-out riverbed, Frank noticed and remarked on a long ridge of washed stone and gravel resembling the casting of a giant earthworm. Cal Renfield explained that this was the waste of gold dredging that had been in profitable operation as late as 1942.

He went on to tell the tale of how in 1859 a group of miners, new to the territory, were thrown out of the gold camp of Tarryall. They pushed on to the South Platte River field and came in with one of the biggest strikes ever made in the area. There they built their own town and named it Fairplay, which still survives today, said Cal Renfield, while Tarryall is dead and gone and all but forgotten.

"Rough if not poetic justice," Frank observed.

"Tell him about Haw Tabor," said Helen from the back seat.

"Haw Tabor was a storekeeper in what was to become Leadville back in the 1870s. At about that time many of the gold workings had been dug out, then somebody discovered that the dark sand the miners had been throwing and cursing because it got in their way was almost pure carbonate of lead and silver. Tabor grubstaked a couple of miners to 17 dollars' worth of groceries and they struck a vein of silver yards wide. Tabor sold his share for a million dollars and with the proceeds went on to make another nine million from other diggings. One of them was the Matchless Mine, which is just about the most famous mine in the entire state."

"And in the end he went broke," Helen said laconically, as if this neatly summed up her philosophy.

"That's right," said her father. "They repealed the Sherman Silver Purchase Act and during the Panic of 1893 silver prices hit rock bottom and Tabor's empire collapsed. When he died in 1899 he was the postmaster in Denver."

They arrived in Radium and stopped at a coffee shop for something to eat. Frank and Helen had a tuna fish salad but Cal Renfield required something more substantial for the inner man: he had grilled steak and french fries with onion rings done in batter. Frank felt like delivering a lecture on polysaturated fats and cholesterol levels but he wisely thought twice about it and decided that it was too late to break the habit of a lifetime.

Afterward they drove out to the hospital, a new, clean, functional, single-story building surrounded by lawns on which sprinklers were playing in the mellow autumn sunshine. It seemed colder here and when Frank remarked on it Cal Renfield pointed out that they had climbed nearly six thousand feet and were now a mile and a half above sea level. Some of the local residents claimed there were only three months to the year at this altitude: "July, August, and Winter."

Dr. Bob Bragg was expecting them. He was a tall lean man, about the same age as Frank, with thinning fair hair that he wore in such a way as to disguise his incipient baldness. His long narrow face bore the marks of worry, the lines on his forehead hardened into a permanent frown as if life were a never-ending series of small battles and minor disappointments. Yesterday had been pretty gruelling, his expression told them, today was about the same, and tomorrow wouldn't be any better.

Cal Renfield introduced Frank as "a fellow journalist," which seemed to be all the explanation Dr. Bragg required for the visit; in any event he accepted it without comment, leading them through into the Isolation Unit which occupied an annex of the hospital, separated from the other wards by two pairs of double-doors. There were twenty-two babies in the Unit, ranging in age from fourteen months down to the latest arrival, a baby girl just nine days old.

They were perfectly normal in appearance, plump, bright eyed, with a healthy sheen to their skin, yet this apparent normality was made to seem incongruous and slightly unsettling by their stillness, silence, and lack of activity. They lay in their cots like perfect mute facsimiles, computerized versions of everything babies were supposed to be except for a vital element that had been omitted from the program—the spark of individuality. There was nothing physically wrong with them that Frank could detect, no signs of mental aberration: they were simply acting as babies with none of the usual signs of babyishness.

"We've carried out all the standard checks on the physiological processes, including the autonomic nervous system, and there's nothing whatsoever wrong with them," Bob Bragg told Frank. "At least nothing that shows up. We've had specialist pediatricians over from Denver and Dr. Samuel Sanborn from the West Coast and none of them know what to make of the syndrome. They're not mentally defective or subnormal—not in any way that we can tell—and there's no case study we can find which deals with this type of condition."

They moved along the row of cots, the passive stare of each child fixed on some imaginary object in the middle distance. Helen had a look of pain on her face as if the spectacle was too harrowing and unnatural, these tiny waxen effigies masquerading as real flesh and blood. There was nothing there, no vital life-force.

"Do they ever cry?" Frank asked.

"Not even at birth," Bob Bragg said, his thin veined hands resting on the rail of a cot. "They're fed regularly of course and they take the food without any trouble, but once when we deliberately delayed the feed by an extra hour not one of them uttered a peep. They just lie there as if they're waiting for something, but don't ask me what it is they're waiting for, I haven't a notion."

"What about the mothers, are they okay?"

"They're upset, naturally. They can see that their baby *looks* all right and they can't understand why it doesn't respond in the usual way. But there's nothing wrong with the mothers healthwise apart from the worry of having given birth to a . . . " He spread his hands, lost for an adequate description.

"Where do you go from here?"

Bob Bragg shrugged his narrow shoulders. It was less a gesture of dismissal as one of hopelessness.

The lines on his forehead were deeply imprinted, the visible trace of a man who had spent many a sleepless night asking himself the same question.

Helen said, "You believe us now?"

"I never doubted your word," Frank replied. "But the fact that what you say is true doesn't necessarily mean that you're right. As Dr. Bragg says, the cause or causes have yet to be identified. If the best pediatricians in the country can't offer a medical opinion as to what's wrong I can't see how Gypsum's ace investigative reporter is going to come up with the answer."

It was rather an unkind jibe and Frank regretted it when he saw Helen's face flush. However, she hadn't treated him with kid gloves and he reckoned that sooner or later she'd have to learn how to take it as well as hand it out; and sooner rather than later wouldn't do any harm.

"I knew all along you were on their side," she came back at him, her face stiff and sullen.

"I'm not on anybody's side, I thought we'd established that," Frank said with some annoyance. "When you can show me a shred of evidence maybe I'll start to take what you say seriously."

Bob Bragg turned to face Helen. "You think you know what's causing this?" he asked mildly. It was implicit in his tone that his question was polite rather than in earnest.

"I have . . . an idea," she said, withdrawing a little, not making it sound too definite.

"Ideas are in short supply around here at the moment."

Helen looked at her father. She said, "Maybe when

111

I've thought about it some more. I don't want to be accused of making accusations without proof."

This was said for Frank's benefit, though she wouldn't look at him.

They walked along the ward, from cot to cot, their footsteps eerily loud in a roomful of silent wide-awake babies. That was another thing, Frank realized, none of them were sleeping—and infants of a few months spent a large part of the day asleep. And it was just as Bob Bragg had remarked, as if they were waiting for something, quite content to bide their time, letting the hours slip away in anticipation of . . . what?

Was it at all possible, as Helen Renfield maintained, that there was some connection between these babies and the Deep Hole Project? She had made the charge blindly, instinctively, with no real evidence to support it, but Frank could have pointed out (if he'd felt so inclined) that that was the way many scientific theoreticians arrived at their most startling and worthwhile concepts. Basing their hypotheses purely and simply on the need to explain something which hitherto had been inexplicable, they made chance guesses—and quite often not even educated ones— at the casual relationship between two apparently unconnected events, worked it all out mathematically on paper, and then left it to the practical scientists, the technicians and research workers to come up with specific observational evidence which proved the hypothesis to be correct. Or incorrect, if that's the way the evidence pointed. But the actual method used was essentially no different from Helen Renfield's: first the unsupported theory followed by proof either for or against.

So how to arrive at a coherent hypothesis which embraced an abundance of antineutrinos flooding in from the center of the Galaxy, atmospheric disturbances leading to freak weather conditions, babies born with none of the normal human attributes and having the appearance of meticulously constructed replicas, men meeting their deaths by unknown causes, and a religious cult which believed the mountain to possess divine significance, to contain some form of dynamic energy which made it in their terms a living entity?

Were these all random occurrences, totally unrelated to each other, or was it possible they were linked in some mysterious fashion? And if so, how? What was the causal (acausal?) relationship which would make sense of such disparate events and draw them together to form a testable hypothesis?

Frank suddenly thought of one possible relationship. It was a crazy idea, but no more crazy, perhaps, than Einstein's suggestion that spacetime was curved. And that had been proved.

The question was, could it be put to the test?

When they reached the door he turned to the doctor. "Do you have an X-ray department in the hospital?"

Bob Bragg confirmed that they had. He smiled wanly. "I know what you're going to say—have we X-rayed them to find out if there's anything wrong with their internal structure? Well we have, Mr. Kersh. On the older infants, not the very young babies for fear of damaging them. Everything was normal, bone structure, main organs, alimentary tract, everything just as it should be and functioning perfectly."

"That's useful to know but in fact I had something else in mind." Frank paused for a moment, considering how best to phrase it. "If you have an X-ray machine then presumably you also have an X-ray dosemeter for detecting the presence of radiation."

Bob Bragg nodded, his permanent frown firmly in place.

"And your staff wear radiation monitoring badges which are checked periodically to see that the level of exposure hasn't gone beyond the critical limit."

"Yes, that's right," the doctor said, apparently mystified.

"Can I ask you to carry out a check while we're here? Place a monitoring badge in one of the cots for fifteen minutes and then run a test on it through the dosemeter. Can you do that?"

"Well . . . yes," said Bob Bragg, blinking. "But what on earth for?"

"To check for radiation."

"Radiation? From where?"

"The babies," Frank said.

Bob Bragg smiled. Then he laughed. "You think they're radioactive?" he said, highly amused.

"You've tested them for everything else, why not see if they're emitting short wavelength electromagnetic waves?"

"It isn't possible."

"You don't know until you try."

"Human beings don't emit X-rays, Mr. Kersh. As you probably know, prolonged exposure to any form of radiation is harmful and can be fatal."

"To human beings," Frank said.

"Yes—" Dr. Bragg broke off and stared at him. He

didn't say anything for several moments; then in a slow subdued tone, "You're seriously suggesting they might be *other* than human?"

Frank shook his head. "Not suggesting, Dr. Bragg, formulating a hypothesis. Would you run the test for me?"

"Very well, if it'll satisfy your curiosity." He pushed open the door and led the way through. "You can wait in my office. I'll have some coffee sent in."

"What made you think of testing them for radioactivity?" Cal Renfield asked when they were waiting in Bob Bragg's office. The doctor had gone off, saying he wouldn't keep them long.

"To be honest, I don't really know," said Frank, being honest. "I think maybe it was something Helen said about trusting your instincts. It suddenly occurred to me that no doctor or pediatrician would ever dream of running a radiation check on a newborn baby, it just wouldn't enter their heads. They've tried everything else and got negative response, so perhaps it's worth a try." He sighed and shook his head. "Crazy notion," he murmured, half to himself.

Helen was watching him, as if at any second amazing revelations were going to issue forth, popping out of his head like cartoon speech balloons. She said:

"Do you believe there is a connection between the babies and what's been happening at the Project? I mean, can you see a scientific reason why the Project should have affected them is this way?"

"Not so far. I'm following your advice and relying on hunches. They could turn out to be skyrockets or damp squibs."

"You know," Helen said, smiling at him faintly, "for the first time I believe you."

"About my hunches?"

"About wanting to find out what's happening. And about not being on their side."

"I'm on nobody's side," Frank told her. "And you have my word, I'm just as mystified as you are about what's going on around here." He pushed his hand through the loose dark-brown curls which surrounded his head like a tangled halo. "I'm supposed to be sitting behind a desk in Chicago," he told himself abstractedly, "not playing scientific detective along Roaring Fork Valley in the middle of Colorado."

The receptionist came in with the coffee. They had just finished drinking it when the door opened and Bob Bragg entered the office. He held a small blue badge with a number printed across it.

They didn't need to ask him about the result of the test: the frown lines printed across his forehead told their own story.

CHAPTER THREE

"Someday you'll make somebody a good wife," Frank said, laying down his fork. "That was the best eezi-freeze TV dinner I've ever tasted."

Helen Renfield, seated across the table from him, raised her wine glass in sardonic salute. "My, my, the way you big-city fellas *do* talk," she said in the coy drawling simper of a mid-West country girl. "Those purty com-pli-ments could sweep a girl right clean off her feet."

Her father wiped his mouth and threw down the napkin. "Helen really looks after me," he told Frank. "Feeds me thick juicy steaks, roast potatoes and blueberry cheesecake as part of my calorie-controlled diet. Without her I'd weigh 160 pounds and look ten years younger."

Frank got up to help Helen clear away the dishes. Cal Renfield sorted through a stack of records and put Sibelius' Symphony No. 2 on the turntable. They sat around the fire drinking black coffee and Salignac five-star French brandy, which Cal Renfield maintained was "my only real indulgence, apart from Havana cigars, fast cars and even faster women."

Helen's mother had died seven years before, when she was fifteen, of the dreaded scourge of Western Civilization: cancer. It had come as a shock to them both and drawn them even more tightly together as a family unit of two. Helen had been planning to go to the University of Colorado but had suddenly changed her mind, and much against her father's wishes had decided to remain in Gypsum, taking on the double chore of keeping house and helping him run the newspaper. She insisted it was what she wanted to do; her motivation wasn't one of pity or maudlin self-sacrifice; she had firmly made up her mind to make a career as a journalist and what better start than on a small-town newspaper? One day she'd try for a newspaper job in Boulder or even Denver itself, but meanwhile she was perfectly happy—and grateful—to be able to learn her trade on the *Roaring Fork Bulletin.*

Frank was accustomed to the new breed of career girl (Chicago was choc-o-bloc with them) and he welcomed it as a healthy sign of female independence, the fact that human potential wasn't being wasted or submerged by the traditional role of wife/mother/housekeeper/general Jack-of-all-trades. At the same time he hated to see women mistaking cold, ruthless—and above all, emotionless—opportunism for genuine emancipation and equality of rights. Many of them felt they had to take on the worst and most aggressive attributes of masculine piggery in order to prove they were as good a man as the next fellow, if not better. But of course they weren't men, they were women, and it saddened him when they shed their natural feminine qualities and became the epitomy

118

of the very thing they were fighting against.

He didn't place Helen Renfield in this category. Her cool demeanor and flip humor he saw as part of the defense mechanism of a young person not at all sure of herself—who she was, where she was going, and what she had to offer the big bustling world outside this Rocky Mountain town. She was far too intelligent (he hoped) to allow the false values of the New Liberated Woman to subvert her own finer sensibilities and the real feminine qualities which she undoubtedly possessed.

This was how Frank Kersh, in his role of amateur social anthropologist, saw her. As Frank Kersh, healthy thirty-three-year-old bachelor with normal libido quotient, he wanted, euphemistically speaking, to sleep with her.

Cal Renfield asked him what he intended to do next, now that his hunch had proved to be correct and the radiation count confirmed as positive. Would he take it up with Professor Friedmann and see what explanation he could offer?

Frank hadn't yet decided what the next step should be. He said, "It still doesn't constitute absolute proof that the Project is to blame. Friedmann could quite easily reject it out of hand—in fact that's probably what he will do—and in a sense he's perfectly right. There still isn't any hard-and-fast evidence to link the babies in the hospital with the neutrino detection experiments being carried out at the Deep Hole Project. They could be entirely unconnected—and we'd have a tough time trying to prove otherwise."

"Strange that babies giving out radioactivity should

119

be cared for in a place called Radium," Helen said.

"It is strange," Frank agreed. "Just one of those odd coincidences that no one can explain. They might easily have been taken to another hospital, in Glenwood Springs maybe, or Lakewood."

"Might have been but weren't," said Cal Renfield, sipping his brandy.

"You're getting to sound like your local preacher— what's he called—Cabel? Delivering gloomy prophesies of doom and disaster from the Book of Genesis. Do you think the people around here really believe in him or do they treat it all as a joke?"

"You want to hear him sometime," Cal Renfield said. "He's pretty impressive. He's got the whole thing worked out." He leaned back at ease in the armchair and clasped his short stubby fingers together across his stomach, as comfortable and content as a cat fed on cream and caviar. "The Telluric Faith states that we're all, each and every one of us, an integral part of the Cosmos. There are different levels of awareness but most people are only aware of the one level they inhabit, what you might call the everyday world. Cabel says that in fact we're part of the living Earth—not living *on* it, you understand, but *part* of it. And as part of the Earth we're also part of the living Sun, and so on up through the various levels to the Cosmic." He frowned and said to Helen, "What's that phrase he uses to describe the different levels?"

"Greater Bodies and Lesser Bodies."

"Right, that's right . . . so if you think of the whole bag of tricks as a gigantic onion, layer upon layer, then our Greater Bodies are the Biotic, the

120

Planetary, Stellar, Galactic, and so on right up to—"
He clicked his fingers and appealed to Helen once
more.

"The Omniverse," she supplied.

"The equivalent of what we'd call the Universe,"
Frank said.

"That's right," Cal Renfield affirmed. "And going
the other way, in descending order, our Inner Bodies
are the Biological, Chemical, Physical, Psychic, and
finally V—which Cabel uses to symbolize the Ultimate Void. You get the overall picture? Each layer
of the onion corresponds to a specific level of awareness, all of which are inter-related. By coincidence
or design, I'm not sure which, human beings come
slap in the middle, with the Omniverse at one ex-
treme and the Ultimate Void at the other."

"Which is another name for the inner self, I take
it?"

"The soul, the astral body, the Id, Ego and Super-
ego, whatever you care to call it. Members of the
Faith believe that all forms of life on Earth are
part of the one conscious intelligence—that's what
Cabel terms the Biotic—and above that we're part
of a greater living body, the Earth, which is itself
part of the Planetary, and so on and so forth. It
obeys the old classical dictum, 'As above, so below,'
each of the different planes in harmony with the
rest."

"You seem to know a lot about it," Frank said,
smiling.

"I've heard the guy often enough, and as I say
he can be fairly convincing when he gets up a full
head of steam."

121

"I remember you telling me that he regards the Telluride Mine as having special significance," Frank said.

"As near as I understand it that has something to do with lines of energy which intersect at various points on the Earth's surface and the Mount of the Holy Cross happens to be situated at one of them." Cal Renfield helped himself to more brandy and offered the bottle to Frank. "What made you think of that?"

Frank poured brandy into his glass, watching the trickle of amber liquid and smelling the heavy rich aroma. He had made up his mind not to tell anyone of his experience underground, but now, well-fed and warmed by five-star French cognac, and with a sympathetic and intelligent audience, he was sorely tempted.

After a moment's silent debate he said, "Everything seems to be centered on the mountain, doesn't it? The Project is based there, the Telluric Faith regard it as being the focal point of their religion, the tremors seem to emanate from that region . . ."

"Those are precisely the things that made us suspicious in the first place," said Helen, leaning forward to take the bottle. She had rolled up the sleeves of her checkered shirt and her arms were smooth and brown, a faint scattering of freckles like flecks of gold dust on her forearms. "There were just too many strange occurrences on that mountain or in some way connected with it—you know, things that didn't make any sense or that we couldn't find an explanation for."

She regarded him seriously, her grey eyes wide

and intent, and Frank had an instant fantasy about the expression those eyes would assume in the act of love-making. He could see them tightening, a little scared and yet eager at the same time, sensuously inviting as a woman's and also naively trusting like those of a young girl.

Had he been seeking proof of thought-transference this might have furnished it, for her cheeks took on a deepening tint and her lips parted slightly, as if she were reading his mind; or it might have been his penetrating gaze which revealed what he was thinking.

Cal Renfield blundered into the mood, oblivious to it, or apparently so, by saying. "The Tellurians could be closer to the mark than they realize."

"In what way?" Frank asked.

"Because of the fault line that runs right along the Valley from Rifle through Eagle and almost as far as Breckenridge. Follows the course of Eagle River for most of the way, then cuts south below the Great Eagle Dam. Hasn't moved an inch since records were kept but it's there right enough. I spoke to a geologist who was doing a survey for the University and he pointed it out on his map. He told me it had been caused by something called the Laramide Revolution which happened 80 million years ago when the Rockies were first formed. There was some kind of colossal upheaval and two mountain ranges were flung up—the Mount of the Holy Cross on one side and Mount Powell on the other. The fault runs between them and eventually, after sixty million years or so, was pushed from both sides and closed up. As I say, there's never been any detectable movement recorded in the vicinity, so maybe it's sealed up good and tight."

Frank nodded. "Which is just as well with the earth tremors you've been having recently."

"What I want to know is what can we *do* about all this?" Helen demanded. She looked at her father and then at Frank. "You say that we need positive proof that the Project is responsible, yet while we're waiting things are getting steadily worse. What do we need to know to convince somebody that we're not just imagining all this, that it's affecting the climate and the terrain and the people in the Valley? I mean—" She held up her hands and curled them into fists, impotent in her frustration "—what would satisfy them? An earthquake? A flood? Some major disaster? Do they want to see the fault crack wide open and all the towns along the Eagle River disappear beneath the crust, wiped from the face of the Earth as if they never existed?"

"Isn't that what Cabel preaches?" Frank said. "Doesn't he prophesy that a Great Flood will one day destroy everything, just as in the Bible?"

"I'm not concerned about Cabel and what he preaches," Helen said brusquely. "I want to know what the hell we can do to stop this before it goes any further. Friedmann must be aware of what's happening, he must realize that these experiments with neutrinos, or whatever they are, are likely to be the cause of a major catastrophe if something isn't done soon to stop them. But how do we get through to him? How do we convince him?" She sounded desperate, not knowing which way to turn.

Frank marvelled how in forty-eight hours he had

come to accept such questions as being valid and in need of urgent answers. Had someone put them to him on his arrival he would have thought that person stupid or crazy, in need of psychiatric treatment. Now he too had grave doubts about the Project and he was as keen as Helen to put a stop to whatever was happening before it was too late. But too late for what? he wondered. Was the Valley threatened by a disaster of some kind, just as the Telluric Faith prophesied? Had the mysterious Mr. Cabel received Divine warning of a supernatural catastrophe that was to strike down from the heavens? But there had to be a rational explanation for all this; he refused to accept that these recent events, however strange and inexplicable, had anything to do with the religious mumbo-jumbo of Greater and Lesser Bodies, Omniverses and Ultimate Voids.

It was just too preposterous.

Cal Renfield heaved himself out of the armchair. He yawned elaborately and flexed his shoulders.

"Think I'll call it a day."

"That's the best thing to call it," Helen said, straight-faced.

"Don't forget to put the cat out."

"We don't have a cat."

"Hell, don't we? What was that I put out last night?"

"The hearth-rug," Helen said. She turned to Frank and said apologetically, "You'll have gathered that this is what passes for sparkling repartee in the Renfield household."

"Don't mind me," Frank said.

Cal Renfield bade them both goodnight and when he'd gone Helen said, "Would you care for some more coffee?"

"It's late. I'd better be going."

"Would you like to stay the night?"

"Thanks, but it's only a short walk to the hotel."

"I know that," Helen said. "I meant with me."

Frank said, "I wasn't aware the Liberation Movement had spread this far West."

It would have been putting it mildly to say that he was taken aback; he'd never been so directly propositioned before. Even with the girl in San Francisco they'd contributed equally to the liaison, each making fifty per cent of the running. He didn't know what to say or what to do with his face.

"The way you looked at me earlier I got the impression you wanted to sleep with me." She made a small inconsequential motion with her shoulders. "Sorry if I got the wrong idea."

"Don't apologize," Frank said swiftly. "I mean yes—I'd like to—it's just that—"

"You're afraid that if we sleep together I won't respect you," Helen said. Her expression was solemn but there was a devilish twinkle in her grey eyes.

Was this, he wondered, the fast come-on before the big put-down? He said, "I just feel rather awkward. After all, it is your father's house."

"But my body," Helen said. She stood up, unbuttoning her shirt, and came to sit beside him on the settee. Her body with lightly tanned and his suspicions that she wasn't wearing a bra were confirmed.

She said, "I don't see what all the hooh-ha is about. I find you very attractive and sexually desirable and the way you looked at me earlier I thought that you felt the same."

Frank nodded dumbly.

"We're both young and healthy," Helen said. "And there isn't a reason in the world why we shouldn't."

"Keep talking," he said, "you're convincing me."

"I think I've done enough talking," Helen said, putting her hand on the nape of his neck. He relaxed under the pressure of her hand and bent forward to kiss her. She tasted sweet, her mouth soft and yielding, and almost immediately he felt her tongue slide between his lips and begin its silky explorations. In the same instant he became hard and the desire for her overpoweringly strong. Unfastening the remaining buttons he slid the shirt from her shoulders and her slim brown arms encircled his neck so that her firm young breasts were lifted and pressed against him.

He said close against her ear, "Yes, I do. I want to fuck you very badly."

"I was hoping you'd do it rather well."

He couldn't help it and laughed out loud and they both fell away from one another, laughing hilariously. He looked at her open mouth, the teeth small and white and perfectly symmetrical, and found it sexually intoxicating; his senses seemed to shimmer and distort, his breath constrained in his chest.

Still watching his face Helen reached out and began to unfasten the buckle on his belt. He touched her face with his fingertips, tracing the fine line as in a delicate pastel drawing, then her lower lip, which

127

he had always maintained was the most sensual part of a woman's anatomy.

"You haven't asked me if I'm married," Frank said.

"Is that the question you're usually asked?" Helen said, unzipping him.

Frank breathed slowly out and nodded. He couldn't trust himself to speak.

"You haven't asked me if I am."

"Are you?" he managed to say.

"No," she said coolly, shaking her head, her eyes not leaving his face.

Frank drew her near to him, a kind of hushed breathless languor pressing down on him. His eyes felt hot. He kissed her, feeling her cool hands fondling him, and behind his closed eyelids he experienced a sensation as though the world had shifted and the trembling in his limbs had communicated itself to everything in the room.

A picture fell off the wall and the house groaned like something alive.

Helen leaped to her feet as the tremor ripped like a shock-wave through the house and the coffee cups and brandy glasses slid off the table and landed in a smashed heap on the carpet. Glowing coals tumbled into the hearth and behind them the window shattered with a sharp crack of a rifle shot. Everywhere there were sounds of breaking glass and falling objects and timbers splintering under the strain. Plaster showered down from the ceiling.

The house was falling apart.

Frank said urgently, "Your father's bedroom, where is it?"

Helen had donned the checkered shirt, her first act of self-preservation, and Frank followed her across the disintegrating living room to the back of the house where they met Cal Renfield in his dressing gown emerging from the bedroom.

He said, "I knew if I didn't make the mortgage payments they'd send the bailiffs in," and pushed Helen and Frank in front of him along a passage and through a small utility room and out into the back graden. The three of them ran around the side of the house into the tree-lined avenue where several people were milling about in confusion and barely controlled panic.

The street light on the corner was leaning at an impossible angle, like a drunk who should fall down but is too intoxicated to realize it.

Frank suddenly thought to make sure his clothes were properly adjusted, and thankfully they were.

"Either that was the first of three," Cal Renfield said, "or it was the big one and we've been let off lightly this once." His dressing gown was a vivid unidentifiable tartan, which made him seem even shorter and more rotund than usual, and rather comical.

"Do they come in threes?" Frank asked.

"Don't most things, especially if they're bad?"

Frank looked along the avenue but it didn't seem as if a great deal of damage had been caused. In the darkness, with only the leaning street lamp for illumination, it was difficult to be sure, though the houses were still intact and there were no large gaping cracks in the sidewalk or the road. It might have felt worse than it really was, he thought, for it didn't require much of a movement—a few inches at most—to crack foundations and shift load-bearing walls off-center. In fact outwardly Cal Renfield's house didn't appear to have suffered serious damage, though several of the windows were broken and from somewhere they could hear the sound of gushing water.

One of the neighbors was counting. He had reached 120 and Cal Renfield said, "I guess that's it for one night. If there was going to be another we should have had it by now. Wouldn't you say so, Clem?"

The neighbor shook his head doubtfully. "Never can tell with these bastards. Just when you've relaxed your guard they hit you with another, right when you're least expecting it. It's like somebody or something is watching and waiting, then when it sees you've let out a sigh of relief—wallop! wham! —catches you bare-assed with your pants around your ankles."

Frank looked away into the darkness, trying to hide a smile, and Helen nudged him in the ribs and whispered, "You're not alone, seems like Clem's had a similar experience."

Cal Renfield was all for going back into the house but the neighbor warned him against it. Frank suggested they walk up to the main square and find out if the hotel had been left unaffected by the tremor.

"You can't stay in the street all night," he pointed out, "and I've a room there with a bed and a couple of armchairs. It's not much but it's better than nothing."

Helen gave him a private look, pursing her lips and pulling a sardonic face.

They were still a fair distance from the square when they heard the low moaning—a faint yet steady drone that reminded Frank of a distant funereal dirge. He had heard it before but couldn't remember where.

Then as they got nearer he did remember: it was the sound that had accompanied the tremor on his first visit to the detection chamber in the depths of the Telluride Mine.

CHAPTER FOUR

Cal Renfield said, "My God, the Tellurians are out in strength tonight."

Frank said, "Are you sure? Is that where the noise is coming from?"

"Nothing like a good old-fashioned thunderstorm or a powerful earth tremor to get them whipped up into a fine old frenzy. Listen for yourself."

Frank did so and gradually began to detect the odd word or phrase through the monotonous mournful wail . . . "prevaileth forty days" . . . "corrupt" . . . "creeping thing" . . .

"Is that the Bible they're quoting?"

"The Book of Genesis."

"Do they believe in the Christian God?"

Cal Renfield, waddling along in his tartan dressing gown, shook his head. "It's a handy piece of scripture to quote from, that's all. Anything that talks about evil and corruption and predicts a cataclysmic end to the world is right up their street."

"What kind of deity do they worship?"

Cal Renfield shrugged. "The Omniverse?"

"More likely the Ultimate Void," Helen suggested drily.

They turned the corner and came in sight of the gathering—over a hundred strong, Frank estimated—grouped around a central figure which was raised above them on a dias of some description. Several of those nearest him carried flaming torches and the scene was at once reminiscent of a Ku Klux Klan meeting, except for the fact, Frank supposed, that none of them wore white pointed hoods.

Yet the face of the leader—Cabel—did seem to be obscured in a way he couldn't quite make out. The flickering torchlight made it difficult to see, and perhaps the hat the preacher wore kept most of his face in shadow, but even so it seemed that his face was covered and that only his eyes and mouth were visible.

The chanting went on, low and intense, filling the air with sonorous vibrations. Cabel remained perfectly still and silent, a tall spare figure dressed in a garment that Frank could only liken to a black one-piece overall, similar to those he had seen technicians wearing in nuclear power plants. It seemed that he was meditating, disengaged from the proceedings, lost and far away and shielded from the gathering by his own inner thoughts.

"How long do they keep this up?" Frank asked.

"I've known them go on for several hours. Once they held a Prayer Meeting on the Mount of the Holy Cross and it didn't finish till dawn. They came back half-frozen and that was in the middle of June." He said out of the corner of his mouth, "Shall we step inside and have a nightcap?"

"I'd like to hear this," Frank said. "You go ahead if you want to."

Cal Renfield went up the steps to the hotel. "Are you coming in?" he asked his daughter.

"I'll stay with Frank. See you later."

She put her arm inside his jacket and huddled close for warmth; there was a perceptible chill in the air now, the cold night air rolling down from the icy peaks. Frank was conscious of her soft warm breasts pressing against him through the thin material of her shirt. He kissed her on the forehead.

"I know, I know," Helen said. "Don't think that I don't feel it too. Damn these Tellurians and their fucking earthquakes."

They listened as the same dirgelike phrases were repeated over and over again. It reminded Frank of a voodoo ceremony in which the participants have to generate a state of self-induced trance, entering into a kind of mindless limbo where the senses are suspended and divorced from reality. He was about to remark on this when for no apparent reason the chanting ceased; it died away to silence and the gathering stood motionless, the torchlight casting a dim smoky light over everything. Near the center of the gathering he caught a sight of a Stetson, a pale blur in the flickering darkness.

Cabel began to speak. At first his voice was toneless, empty of feeling, but as he went on it gathered force and stridency, the words echoing flatly from the fronts of the buildings surrounding the square. And as Cal Renfield had said, it was curiously hypnotic.

"And V saw that the wickedness of man was great in the earth, and that every imagination of the

134

thoughts of his heart was only evil continually. And it repented him that he had made man on the earth, and it grieved him at his heart.

"And V said, I will destroy man whom I have created from the face of the earth; both man, and beast, and the creeping thing, and the fowls of the air; for it repenteth me that I have made them.

"And V looked upon the earth and, behold, it was corrupt; for all flesh had corrupted his way upon the earth. And V said, The end of all flesh is come before me; for the earth is filled with violence through them; and behold, I will destroy them with the earth.

"And, behold, I, even I, do bring a flood of waters upon the earth, to destroy all flesh, wherein is the breath of life, from under heaven; and every thing that is in the earth shall die.

"And it came to pass after seven days that the waters of the flood were upon the earth. And the rain was upon the earth forty days and forty nights.

"And the flood was forty days upon the earth; and the waters increased, and the waters prevailed exceedingly upon the earth; and all the high hills, that were under the whole heaven, were covered. Fifteen cubits upward did the waters prevail; and the mountains were covered.

"And all the flesh died that moved upon the earth, both of fowl, and of cattle, and of beast, and of every creeping thing that creepeth upon the earth, and every man: All in whose nostrils was the breath of life, of all that was in the dry land, died.

"And every living substance was destroyed which was upon the face of the ground, both man, and cattle, and the creeping things, and the fowls of the heaven; and they were destroyed from the earth.

"And the waters prevailed upon the earth a hundred and fifty days."

There was something about his voice, a certain quality, which disturbed Frank. In an odd way it was similar to the feeling of *déjà vu*—the sudden shock of recognition that one has lived through the same experience before when it is plainly impossible for this to have happened. Perhaps it was the words themselves that were familiar. And yet there was something more than that . . . something at the back of his mind that he couldn't quite bring into focus.

He said to Helen, "Who is this man Cabel? Where is he from?"

"Take your pick," Helen said. "I've heard at least five different versions of who he is and where he comes from. Some people say he used to work the Telluride Mine all on his own before the Project moved in, which is why he preaches against it. Then there's the story that he was one of the construction engineers on the Great Eagle Dam who received a vision from the Ultimate Void that it was evil and would one day be destroyed. Walt Stringer believes him to be the embodiment of the spirit that lives in the mountain—a spirit of the living Earth in human form. Some of the people around here really believe in such things. Maybe it's a leftover from the old Indian legends, the belief in ancient spirits inhabiting rocks and caves and rivers."

"Which version gets your vote?"

"I've never thought about it." Her hand tightened around his waist. "I prefer real flesh and blood to ancient spirits."

Cabel was saying, "We have warned them, brethren. We have said that the Earth will cast them out and seal up its secret places. They do not listen. We have said that the desecration of the holy mountain will bring death and destruction onto their own heads and all their profane works. Still they refuse to listen. But now the Earth speaks for us with a tongue of lightning and a voice of thunder, and in the depths of the Earth the power of the Ultimate Void moves and shakes the puny works of man, and there is no man who does not feel its anger and know fear in his heart."

"Does he write his own material?" Frank said.

"Keep your voice down," Helen warned him. "The members of the Faith can get a bit touchy if they hear you mocking their leader."

"And they really believe all this?"

"If someone prophesies disaster and it looks like it's coming true, then naturally the people start listening to him and taking notice of what he says. Cabel was spouting this stuff long before the storms and the tremors began. At first everyone thought he was a raving madman but then things started to happen just the way he predicted—and it doesn't take many freak thunderstorms and earth tremors to change people's views."

"Is that true?" Frank asked. "Did he actually predict the freak weather conditions before they began?"

"Over two years ago."

"About the time the Project started up."

"Yes."

" . . . but the time is nigh, brethren, when the unbelievers shall reap the seeds of their unbelief. Even now as I speak the power of the Ultimate Void is stirring in the depths of the holy mountain. We have all felt its warning; we know that soon, very soon, its wrath will be unleashed, and then will come the final day of reckoning when the flood waters will rise up and sweep away forever these heathens who commit sacrilege in the name of science against the sacred Omniverse. They seek to learn its secrets, to comprehend the elemental forces which span the Cosmos, but they are as ignorant fools, no better than mischievous children, tampering with a structure beyond their conception.

"We of the Telluric Faith—the only true and faithful inhabitants of this planet, the only true believers in this sentient Earth—we, the Tellurians, are witness to the folly and greed and blind stupidity of that species of creeping thing which creepeth upon the face of the ground and is not worthy of the living Earth. They have ignored our preaching, as even now they ignore the warning of the Ultimate Void, and it is upon them and their children that the waters of heaven will descend, and bear them away, and the breath of life will be taken from them, and they will be destroyed from the living Earth for evermore . . ."

"I can understand how he gets them going," Frank said. "Another ten minutes of this and I'll be asking to join."

"Have you heard enough?"

"I reckon so, country girl. Take me to your boudoir."

138

They turned to mount the steps of the hotel and somebody was standing in the shadow of the porch, barring their way. A large hand the color and consistency of red sandstone spread itself across Frank's chest as he tried to step forward, halting him in mid-stride. It was as though he'd walked into a barn door.

"You shouldn't mock what you don't understand," Chuck Strang said. His immaculate white Stetson was tipped forward so that his narrow squinting eyes looked down on them from beneath the curling brim. He had plenty of opportunity to look down on them, standing six feet six in his cowboy boots, and the uncomfortable thought passed through Frank's mind that even without them he must have been a good three inches above six feet.

"You shouldn't talk so loud," Chuck Strang admonished him. "You never know who might be listening. For somebody who's a stranger in this town you sure do have a big mouth."

Frank didn't think it wise to correct him on such a small item of physical description; after all, he reasoned, perhaps he did have a big mouth.

Helen said, "I thought I'd mentioned it before, Strang. The part of John Wayne's saddlebag has already been cast." She turned to Frank apologetically, "You'll have to excuse him, we had the bolt in his neck tightened yesterday."

"Is that meant to be humorous?" Chuck Strang inquired.

"Be careful there, Chuck, that was a three-syllable word you used. Next thing we know you'll be learning to read without moving your lips."

Frank wished she wouldn't do all the tough talking

for him. In fact he wished she wouldn't do any talking at all. A man built like a bear who spent his leisure moments hog-tying Brahman bulls wouldn't need to expend much effort dealing with a soft-living city-boy who only got callouses from sitting around all day.

He said, intending it seriously, "If I offended your religious feelings, I apologize. What you choose to believe is your business. I'm only sorry that you overheard me."

"I bet you are," Chuck Strang said. He nodded slowly but he wasn't smiling. "And I guess you think that makes everything all right. You say your little piece, as if that makes everything sweet and easy, and then hustle Little Miss Hot-Ass into the hotel for a quick lay. Is that the idea? Is that what you had in mind?"

Frank felt he ought to object to Chuck Strang's implication and the slur it cast on Helen, but he was rather circumspect in the way he should set about expressing it. He didn't want to rile the man.

Helen folded her arms defiantly and faced the tall sunburned rancher in the white Stetson and silver spurs. "Why don't you get it off your chest, Strang, and tell him that this town isn't big enough for the both of you? Then we'll say goodnight and leave you with the rest of these—"

"Helen!" said Frank warningly. "He's entitled to his religious beliefs."

"Is that what they are?" she responded caustically. "Looks to me more like grown men trying to whip up enough Dutch courage to form a lynching party."

Frank groaned inwardly.

"The trouble is, Strang," Helen went relentlessly on, "we've all seen the same B movie at least a million times. And the plot still stinks."

"I think we'll just be on our way," Frank said, making as if to move into the hotel.

"I think maybe you won't," said Chuck Strang, standing in his way. "I also think the members of the Faith might like to know we have a real living scientist right here in our midst." For no reason he pushed Frank hard in the chest.

It was the first indication that this wasn't just plain bravura after all; Chuck Strang wasn't play acting, he was in deadly earnest, and Frank began to get the unwelcome feeling that he would have to do some fast talking or even faster running to extricate himself from what was becoming a tense situation. Helen's diplomatic remark about a lynching party hung in his mind, like a Ku Klux Klan cross burning vividly against a black night sky.

He said, somewhat wearily. "You've got it wrong, Strang. I'm not a scientist. I'm a journalist. I write for a science magazine."

"You're connected with that thing over on the mountain."

"Who told you that?"

"Mr. Cabel."

Frank stared at him. He almost smiled. "The preacher told you that?" he said, bewildered. "He doesn't know anything about me."

"He knows you right enough. He says you're connected with the Project. He told us all, the night of the storm."

Frank recalled the meeting that had been held in

the square the night the power had failed. But what was all this about Cabel telling the members of the Faith that he was a scientist working on the Project? He'd never met the man, and as far as he knew Cabel didn't even know that somebody called Frank Kersh existed. Unless Stringer had told him. That must be it, Frank guessed, unable to understand how else it could have happened. The hotel manager had taken him for a scientist and passed the word along to Cabel. Nothing else made sense; and yet he was still uneasy. Why should Cabel single him out and think it worth telling the members of the Telluric Faith that he was actively engaged on the Project? He wasn't a threat to them, and there was no earthly reason why Cabel should think him worthy of special attention.

He became aware that the preacher's sermon had ended and that close behind him a silent watching group had formed. The only sound was the soft crackling flare of the torches.

Helen said, "This is stupid. Are you going to let us through, Strang?"

Chuck Strang said, "What's the rush, Helen, can't you wait to get in the sack with this heretic?"

"My, how your vocabulary has improved. Two months ago you'd have thought heretic was some rare form of cattle disease." She stood, arms folded, one hip thrust out, in the manner of a schoolteacher having to deal with a particularly dull and recalcitrant pupil.

Frank was beginning to wish he'd kept up with his karate lessons.

Then Chuck Strang said in a low intense voice,

"You'd better tell your friends, Kersh, that next time the mountain won't be content with only four human sacrifices. That was just a gentle warning. Next time it's going to take all of you, every last one. You think the mountain is a heap of dead rock but that's where you're mistaken. The mountain is part of the living Earth, just as Mr. Cabel says, and it's waiting for you, biding its time. Tell them people up there that if they don't clear out the mountain is going to split clean in half and swallow them and their Project whole."

His eyes had the depth and fixed intensity of a madman's stare. He had gone beyond the point where reasoned argument would have made the slightest difference; Frank knew that anything he might say would never get through that solid, impenetrable wall of fervent religious conviction. Chuck Strang believed in the doctrine Cabel preached: the scales had fallen from his eyes and he was a true and passionate believer in the living reality of the Ultimate Void.

"Is that the message you want me to pass on to them?" Frank said.

"They've got forty-eight hours. Either they leave for good or they stay there—forever."

"Amen," Helen said boredly.

CHAPTER FIVE

The compound was deserted and there was a strangely subdued air about the place, as if, Frank thought, last night's tremor had shocked them into silence and inactivity. He wondered whether more damage had been caused to the underground installation. In many ways this could be even more dangerous than the flooding of the lower level—weakening the support structures so that a relatively minor disturbance could block the tunnels and shaft, sealing the men below ground in a granite tomb.

As he was parking the Toronado Helen remarked on how quiet everything was, adding, "Perhaps they've heeded Chuck Strang's warning and cleared out."

"I doubt it. Neither Friedmann or Leach seem to give a hang about what the local people think. Their sole interest is in conducting scientific research; anything else doesn't rate a mention."

Is it really beyond all possible doubt that the experiments are completely harmless? Isn't it just feasible that they've triggered off something in the atmosphere—some kind of weird side-effect the

144

scientists never expected and are totally unaware of?"

Frank meditated for a moment, pressing his fingertips against his closed eyelids. He said, "When I arrived in Gypsum I could have answered those questions without a second's hesitation. There was absolutely no shadow of a doubt in my mind. Now I'm not at all sure. After what I've seen and heard these past three days it's pretty obvious that something—I don't know what the hell it is—that something connected with the Deep Hole Project is going seriously wrong." He turned to look at her. "As far as my knowledge of astrophysics goes, Helen, there is no known particle reaching the Earth from outer space that has any kind of adverse effect, either on animals, plants, human beings, the Earth itself. We're being bombarded with literally billions of particles every second of the day and night and as far as we know they either interact with other particles and are absorbed, or else they pass harmlessly through the Earth—through us too—as if we weren't here."

He thought of the antineutrinos from the galactic center that Friedmann and his team had detected and it was on the tip of his tongue to add a corollary to his previous statement to the effect that an increase in antineutrinos by a factor of two hundred might just be the one exception to the rule. But he had given his word that he wouldn't reveal the information to anyone until Friedmann and Leach had had time to discuss it and reach a decision; so he resisted the temptation and said nothing. But he was conscious that time was running out for the Project, and not only because of the threats issued by the Tellurians. The storm was gathering in more ways than the meteorological—he could sense it everywhere, a dreadful foreboding in the atmosphere that was as tangible as a physical if unseen presence.

They walked across the dusty red compound to the hut which housed Professor Friedmann's office and were about to enter when the door was abruptly wrenched open and they were confronted by Dr. Leach. The shock of his grotesque appearance, this small ill-made man framed in the doorway, took Helen aback and she gasped involuntarily.

His thatch of thick black hair and his dark-eyed gaze seemed to add emphasis to his deformed stature, almost as if nature had bestowed these attributes to draw attention to her botched handiwork. He said roughly:

"What are you doing here, Kersh? I thought we agreed that you'd await our decision."

"That's right, we did." Frank looked down on the dark stunted man in the white lab coat blocking the doorway. "I'd like to see Professor Friedmann."

"Why?"

"There are a couple of things I want to discuss with him. Recent events have altered the situation. And I think he ought to know how the people of Gypsum are reacting; there could be trouble."

Leach studied him for a long moment, his eyes hard and suspicious beneath the single dark bar of his eyebrows. Helen had moved closer to Frank, intimidated by his aggressive manner and physical appearance.

Dr. Leach said, "You can't see him, it isn't possible."

"Is he here?"

"I've said you can't see him. Isn't that plain enough?"

"If he's here I insist on seeing him. It's important." Frank stared into his eyes, meeting his look squarely, refusing to let the man's hostility frighten or get the better of him.

"What is it you wish to say to him? Tell me and I'll pass the message along."

"That won't do."

"It will have to do."

"Is he underground in the detection chamber?" Frank asked, glancing toward the head of the shaft. "If so, I'll wait. I'm not going anywhere."

"You're leaving. Right now. Professor Friedmann isn't here, so there's no point in you staying."

"Okay," Frank agreed amiably. "If the Professor isn't here, where is he? I take it you know how to reach him."

Leach looked away, his eyes flickering, almost as if he were unsure what to do next. He licked his wide lips and a tiny muscle jumped above his left eye.

Helen had apparently overcome her trepidation, for she said, "We haven't come all the way up here to be fobbed off with a weak excuse. It's very important that we see Professor Friedmann urgently. If you know where he is it's in everyone's interests that you tell us. We must speak with him."

Leach seemed to waver momentarily, the same shifting glance of uncertainty appearing in his eyes; then he shook his head defiantly. "You'll have to leave. When the Professor returns I'll ask him to call you at your hotel. I'm not asking, I'm telling you to leave, right this minute."

147

"Suppose we don't intend to?" Frank said. He was surprised by a slow beating pulse of anger building up inside. It was the anger of frustration, of meeting threats and blank refusals wherever he went, and it was compounded by the nagging irritation that everyone but him was privy to secrets which if revealed and brought together would make sense of this whole bizarre business. Why was Leach so anxious to prevent him seeing Professor Friedmann? And if the Professor wasn't here, where was he? Leach himself didn't seem sure about anything.

But the small deformed man was sure about one thing. He said in his harsh grating voice, "If you don't get off, Kersh, I'm going to have you thrown off. I'll have them strap you and your girlfriend in that fancy red car of yours and roll you back down the mountain. And don't think I won't do it."

"I don't think he wouldn't do it," Helen said nervelessly.

Frank wished that at moments like these she wouldn't choose to indulge herself in slick verbal repartee. She had an acute mind and a keen intelligence but on occasion he would have preferred it if she kept her mouth shut.

As if to back up his threat Leach had brought his hands out of the pockets of his white coat. They were large and powerful and covered in dark hair, made to seem more capable of a cruel strength by being so disproportionate to the rest of him.

Frank said quietly, "You have a short memory, Dr. Leach."

Leach fixed him with his dark stare. "What do you mean by that?"

"We have an agreement, remember? You gave me certain information which I promised not to reveal. But since then the situation has changed, and if you still refuse to allow me to see Professor Friedmann you leave me no alternative but to break that agreement. I can be back in Chicago by this evening and I'm sure my editor will find space for the story in the next issue."

Leach reacted with a speed and suddenness that left him unprepared, with no time to avoid the blow which knocked the breath from his body: he went down on his back in the red dust, winded and gasping, and Leach came after him with single-minded ferocity, snarling with rage and anger.

Frank rolled away, still shocked by the unexpected attack, and only just made it to his feet when Leach came at him again, swinging his large hairy fists with murderous intent. There was a moment—a split-second—when Frank registered the look in the man's eyes, and it reminded him of the glazed expression of madness in Chuck Strang's eyes, the same burning intensity and absolute unwavering purpose. He thought: These people are being driven insane. They're losing contact with reality, living in dreams and haunted by demented visions—

But it wasn't a good time for psychological analysis.

He stepped quickly to one side as Leach lunged at him and by no more than a fraction of time and space avoided another blow to the stomach. Then they were grappling ineffectively in a parody of a brawl, kicking up clouds of red dust, and Frank knew that if Leach managed to get one good swing at him it would all be over. The man's arms and shoulders were powerfully made, compensating for his small stature, and he had the strength of someone in the grip of blind frenzy.

They scuffled about, Frank not releasing his hold, their legs becoming entangled so that they fell and rolled together, Leach struggling to extricate himself. Frank managed to get his fingers around the man's throat, no longer concerned about anything but the act of self-preservation, forgetting everything in the desperate struggle to survive. It was the most basic of all animal instincts, the need to protect oneself from attack, and he gripped the man's throat with every ounce of strength he possessed. But Leach didn't seem to be aware that he was being slowly strangled, even though there were flecks of foam at the corners of his mouth: he lashed out wildly and caught Frank a blow to the temple which seemed to jar his skull and reverberate through his brain and he felt his hand loosening and slipping away, his fingers weak and rubbery as if filled with warm glycerine.

He was dazed and insensible to his surroundings, his faculties all adrift, lost in a swirling mist that fogged his eyes and ears. His head roared.

Time fled away and he wondered if he was unconscious. He couldn't be dead (it was unlikely) because his stomach was hurting where Leach had first hit him. He was probably unconscious, he decided, which under the circumstances wasn't a bad condition to be in; better than being beaten to a pulp by a demented dwarf with the hands of an ape grafted onto the ends of his arms.

He was quietly contemplating who might have performed the operation when a voice, clear and distinct and close to his ear, said:

"Next time we'll find a phone booth and you can change into your cape and boots."

Frank said hazily, "What happened, did you hit him with something?"

"Not me," Helen said. "I'm the type of girl who stands idly by during a fight and bites her knuckles."

Frank opened his eyes and the world was still there, much as he'd left it, except that Lee Merriam and two other men were holding Dr. Leach, pinning his arms behind his back. Lee Merriam saw that Frank was conscious and bent over him, asking how he felt.

"Sickly," Frank replied truthfully.

"My hero," Helen said, and with Lee Merriam's help got him to his feet.

Leach had quieted down, though his eyes were intensely dark and brooding in his broad pale face. There was a gleam of spittle on his chin.

"What happened?" asked Lee Merriam.

"I think you ought to put that question to him," Frank said. "I wanted to see Professor Friedmann and when I insisted he became what you might call violent."

"Without putting too fine a point on it," Helen said. "Professor Friedmann isn't here."

"I'm slowly beginning to accept that fact. Where is he, do you know?"

"We're not sure. He could be underground."

"He *could* be? Don't you know?"

"We're trying to locate him. He was seen early this morning but we're not sure if he went down to the detection chamber or not. Everyone who goes underground is supposed to make an entry in the log; either the Professor didn't make an entry or he's gone off somewhere without telling anyone."

"It's important that I speak to him as soon as possible," Frank said. He massaged his stomach muscles and winced.

"Do you feel all right?"

"No," Frank said. "But with sympathetic care and understanding I should pull through."

Lee Merriam turned to the two men. "Take Dr. Leach to the sick bay. Tell Smitty what happened and ask him to give the Doctor a shot to calm him down. And stay with him," he added. He turned back and said in a low voice, "Come into the office, I want to talk to you."

They stepped inside the hut and went into Professor Friedmann's office.

Lee Merriam said, "Shut the door." He went to a filing cabinet and took out a blue folder, opened it and gave Frank a typewritten sheet to read. He said, "I'm breaking all the rules, but to be honest with you I don't know what to do next. We can't locate the Professor and Dr. Leach has been behaving strangely."

"We noticed," Helen said drily.

"I need to discuss this with somebody," Lee Merriam went on, "and you seem the only guy around who might have a clue as to what's happening."

Frank tried to laugh but quickly decided against it when his stomach seized up with cramp. He glanced at the piece of paper, his expression of curiosity slowly changing to one of puzzled consternation.

"What is it?" Helen said.

"Autopsy report."

Lee Merriam nodded grimly. "On the four men who were killed underground." He waited a moment and said, "What do you make of it?"

Frank shook his head. "I don't know." He looked at Lee Merriam. "All four died of *brain* tumors?"

"I thought they drowned," Helen said, frowning and glancing from one to the other.

"That was the story we put out," Lee Merriam said. "Read the rest of it," he told Frank. "It gives the probable cause of the tumors consistent with the pattern of growth and taking into account the medical histories of the four men. I think with 'probable cause' he's hedging his bets. It's just that he doesn't want to come straight out and say it."

"Say what?" Helen asked, becoming impatient.

Frank read the concluding paragraph of the report out loud:

" 'In my opinion the probable cause of such severe damage to the cerebrum and cerebral cortex would seem to be as a result of high-intensity radiation over a relatively short period of time—hours or at the most days, rather than weeks or months. It isn't possible to specify the type of radiation, nor its source, though no doubt this could be deduced from further analysis of damaged brain tissue in a suitably equipped research laboratory.' "

"They died of radiation sickness?" Helen said.

"They died of brain tumors caused by a high dose of radiation, as yet unspecified," Frank corrected her. He handed the sheet back to Lee Merriam. "We know of one possible source—the chlorine-37 in the tanks decay into argon-37 when a neutrino interacts with it. And argon-37 is radioactive."

"That's true," Lee Merriam said. "But as I understand it the level is so low that they have trouble detecting it at all. They have to let it build up in the tanks and flush it out with helium. Even then there's hardly much more than that given out by a luminous watch."

"So it doesn't seem as though the detection tanks were the source."

Lee Merriam shook his head. He closed the blue folder and returned it to the filing cabinet. "The mine is as clean as a whistle. We received this report yesterday morning and I went down with a counter and checked it out personally. There's not a whisper. How can four men be subjected to a fatal dose of radiation when they're shielded by over a mile of solid rock? You could detonate a hydrogen bomb on the mountain and providing the shaft was sealed good and tight the fall-out wouldn't affect them. How in hell—"

He swept his arms wide in a gesture of bewildered defeat.

"What did Professor Friedmann make of the report?"

"I'll tell you the truth, Frank it isn't only Karl Leach who's flipped his lid round here. Lately both he and the Professor have been acting weird. It's as if they know something—some kind of secret—and they're doing everything they can to keep it from the rest of us. When I asked Professor Friedmann about the report he just ignored me, didn't even bother to reply. I said shouldn't we notify the Institute of Astrophysics and he told me to mind my own business. He said I wasn't a member of the scientific staff and it was none of my concern how he chose to run the station. In the past he's always been a pretty

154

accommodating sort of a guy but in the last few weeks things have certainly changed. I don't know what to make of it all or what I should do about it."

He folded his arms and stared through the small window at the bright orange latticework of girders supporting the winding gear. His eyes had the absent fretful look of a deeply worried man.

"I think the first thing we should do is find Professor Friedmann," Frank said. "Are you in communication with the detection chamber?"

Lee Merriam nodded. "But there's no one answering, which doesn't tell us very much."

"Then you'd better send somebody down."

"I already have." He looked at his watch. "The electric track hasn't been repaired on the lower level, so it's going to take them some time to reach the detection chamber. I should know something within an hour."

"And if he isn't there?"

Lee Merriam pursed his lips while he considered this. "I guess there's no option. I'll have to call the Institute and report on the situation and ask them to send a team out here. With the Project leader missing and his assistant in no fit condition, that's about all I can do."

Helen caught Frank's eye. She said quietly, "Yesterday the babies at the hospital, today the four men who were killed in the mine. Is that the link you've been searching for?"

"You mean the radiation?" Frank said, "It's a link, all right, but you tell me what it means. These men died from it and yet the babies seem to thrive on it almost as though it were a form of nutrition. There's

155

a connection sure enough, it's just that we don't know where the radiation is coming from and what's causing it."

"Are those the kids that have been born over the past two years?" Lee Merriam asked. "The ones in Radium?"

"That's right. We went to look at them yesterday. You've heard about them?"

Lee Merriam went to the filing cabinet and pulled out a fat file of newspaper clippings, which he dumped on the desk. "Every report on those kids since the day the first one was born. Professor Friedmann had his secretary comb every newspaper within a fifty mile radius of here for items on them. There's also a complete list of their parents' names and addresses, the date each kid was born, and how they're progressing. Every last detail is right here."

"Did he say why he was so interested in them?" Frank asked.

"Guilt complex," Helen said, her eyes flat and cold.

"No, he didn't give a reason, and it never occurred to me to ask him," Lee Merriam admitted. "You know what scientists are like, they live in a closed world and tend to do things that non-scientists find inexplicable, even a little weird sometimes."

"Ain't that the living truth," Helen said with heavy sarcasm.

Frank looked at the folder on the desk and then at Lee Merriam. "We'd better find Professor Friedmann," he said. "Looks like he's got some explaining to do."

They drove back to Gypsum and Frank dropped Helen off at the newspaper office. He made her promise that the *Bulletin* wouldn't run the story on what had caused the death of the four scientists until they'd had the chance to talk to Professor Friedmann and find out what explanation he had to offer.

"You bend over backwards to be fair, don't you, Frank?" Helen said in a tone that was more accusing than complimentary.

"I don't want to be responsible for wholesale panic in this town. Imagine what the Telluric Faith would make of this if they got to hear about it. Let's at least give Friedmann the opportunity to put forward his side of the story." He added meaningfully, "The press does have a responsibility not to alarm the populace unnecessarily."

"Which shouldn't outweigh its responsibility to publish the truth," Helen retorted. She ducked back in the car and kissed him on the mouth.

"Is that a bribe?" he asked her.

"In lieu of services yet to be rendered."

"I'll add it to your account."

"It'll be paid in full," she promised him, and skipped across the sidewalk into the office.

He drove along the main street and parked outside the Cascade Hotel. Again he was struck by the normality of everything: it didn't seem feasible that beneath the fabric of this quiet, orderly, ostensibly peaceful community there should lurk the paranoia of religious fanaticism. And yet, as Frank had to admit to himself, it was no less incredible than what had been happening at the Deep Hole Project—men who died of brain tumors caused by radiation, scientists who disappeared without warning or who were suddenly transformed into violent raving madmen. All of this had to fit together somehow; all these events formed a pattern that either he was too ignorant to understand or too dense to see.

As for black vibrating objects which had the power to transport human beings through 150 feet of solid rock . . . he preferred to suspend his rational faculties for the time being and postpone final judgment. There was quite a few things not dreamed of in his philosophy, Frank realized, and he wasn't going to compound ignorance with rank stupidity.

Part of the square was flooded with a burst main, the aftermath of the previous night's tremor, and a gang of workmen was hard at work in a trench, lowering new sections of pipe into position.

Frank went through into the lobby. Spencer Tutt was behind the desk, propped on his elbows in his usual posture of lackadaisical indifference, his lean chest and jutting shoulders as spare as a scarecrow's. With what seemed great and wearisome effort he

158

raised himself upright and reached behind him into a pigeonhole.

"Cable arrived for you, Mr. Kersh. 'Bout half hour ago. Didn't know where you could be reached."

Frank took it, nodding his thanks. He said, "Can I get something to eat around here?"

Spencer Tutt sucked on a tooth and shook his head. "Dining room won't be open till tonight. There's a coffee shop along the street. Get a meal there or a sandwich. They stay open all day."

Frank turned away and Spencer Tutt went on, "Are you plannin' to stay on here, Mr. Kersh? I'm only askin', you understand, 'cos Walt Stringer was wonderin'. He asked me to ask you."

"At fifteen dollars a night I'd have thought he'd be glad of all the business he can get."

Spencer Tutt shrugged lazily. "I'm only doing what he told me."

"Tell Mr. Stringer from me that when I'm ready to leave I'll let him know." He smiled without using his eyes. "All right?"

"Sure 'nough, Mr. Kersh. I'll tell him that."

Frank went along the street to the coffee shop and sat in a corner booth, ordering Chicken Maryland with a side salad, fruit salad and cream, and black coffee. While he waited for it to be served he opened the cable, lit a cigarette, and concentrated on what Fred Lockyer had to tell him about the latest theoretical research data on neutrinos. When the meal arrived he had read it through once and was about to read it again; Fred Lockyer must have thought it important enough not to economize on the telegram charge, nor to spare the smallest detail. It was all here, in terse technical shorthand that stretched Frank Kersh's knowledge of high-energy particle physics to the utmost. But he grasped the basic essentials, and those were precisely what he needed to know to complete the picture.

It was a picture at once simple and complex: the simplicity lay in the lucid theoretical reasoning while the difficulty arose out of the failure of the everyday imagination to visualize events on a subnuclear scale. The layman's conception of atomic structure was, needless to say, erroneous. Most people still thought of the atom as being comprised of a series of billiard balls circling around the nucleus, much as the planets of the solar system orbit the Sun. It was a model which led to a host of false assumptions, not to mention the layman's confusion in failing to understand that the atomic nucleus was, by definition, incapable of being visualized *at all* in terms that the human mind could comprehend. It was on such a vastly different scale to that which human beings were used to that it was literally impossible to construct a model by employing objects and artifacts within common experience. Therein lay the difficulty—the ultimate conceptual unknowableness of what constituted the stuff on matter and energy.

The theoretical structure, on the other hand, was capable of being understood by anyone with a scientifically trained mind who was used to dealing with abstract mathematical symbolism and visualizing concepts in terms of pure logic and deductive reasoning.

The cable spelled it out:

Recent experiments at Fermilab near Chicago had produced surprising and totally unexpected results.

The scientists had fired a barrage of neutrinos at a 400-ton block of steel and the ensuing interaction had brought forth a shower of hadrons which had been absorbed by the surrounding material. So far so good: just what current theory predicted would happen. Then out of the energy created by the collision came three long-range particles known as *muons*—which not only hadn't been predicted but for which there was no tenable explanation. It had been known for some time that neutrinos decayed into *muons* upon interaction with other particles, but to have produced three of them from a single neutrino was, to say the least, puzzling.

These events—the generation of three simultaneous particles from the one interaction—had been dubbed *trimuons*, and even now the theoreticians were busily engaged in trying to formulate a new hypothesis of nuclear generation to account for them.

This information in itself was interesting but not particularly enlightening with regard to the experiments being carried out at the Deep Hole Project. If *trimuon* events had been detected by Friedmann's team there was no reason to suppose they would be any more harmful than those generated artificially at Fermilab.

It was the second part of the cable, dealing with the anti-particle equivalents of neutrinos, that cleared away the fog and for the first time gave Frank Kersh a real insight into what had been taking place at the bottom of the Telluride Mine. Fred Lockyer was here entering the realms of speculative prediction, but nonetheless his assumptions were still firmly based on the premises which had been established for many years and accepted by high energy physicists the world over.

He postulated what would happen if the neutrino-*trimuon* interaction was interpreted as an antineutrino-*antitrimuon* event. That was all. He simply transferred the same theoretical framework as it applied to the ordinary world of matter to the extraordinary world of anti-matter. His conclusion was that a stream of antineutrinos travelling at the speed of light would, upon hitting the target, decay into *antitrimuons* and produce vast amounts of energy which would be released in the form of radiation. This of course had never been attempted in the laboratory for the simple reason that it was a highly-dangerous experiment and would generate enough lethal radiation to contaminate not only the laboratory but the surrounding countryside for a radius of a hundred miles.

His concluding thought was one of cheerful reassurance to the effect that antineutrinos didn't exist in nature in sufficient numbers to pose a threat to the Earth. Neutrinos outnumbered them by "a trillion to one" and he had worked it out mathematically that under normal circumstances an antineutrino-*antitrimuon* interaction would occur only once in every ten thousand events. Since antineutrinos were comparatively rare, and the rate of interaction so small, there was absolutely no chance that any significant amount of radiation would be generated by the stray antineutrino which happened to collide with a suitable target and decay into an *antitrimuon.* The odds against this happening were, as he put it, "infinitesimal."

But then Fred Lockyer wasn't aware that for the

past two years the Solar Neutrino Detection Station near Gypsum, Colorado had been detecting a 200-fold increase in antineutrinos reaching the Earth from the center of the Galaxy.

And what was even more critical, as Frank now realized, was the fact that the local geophysical strata was ideally suited to producing antineutrino-*antitrimuon* interactions: the Mount of the Holy Cross was composed largely of tellurous ore which made it in effect a 14,000-feet-thick target area for the antineutrinos flooding in from outer space. It was nature's equivalent of Fermilab's 400-ton block of steel—only a million times bigger. Add to that the mile-deep strata beneath and you had the most perfect conditions imaginable for antineutrino-*antitrimuon* decay—producing vast floods of radiation which without doubt had been responsible for the deaths of the four scientists.

And much else besides.

The Chicken Maryland had cooled and finally congealed on the plate. He had chain smoked three cigarettes in under ten minutes and had read and reread the cable so many times he knew it by heart.

Had he at last found the answer to what had been causing the mysterious chain of circumstances along the Roaring Fork Valley? The more he thought about it, the more plausible it became:

Severe atmospheric turbulence.

Freak thunderstorms.

Earth tremors.

Scientists killed by radiation.

Irrational behavior by the Project leader and his assistant.

The Telluric Faith—question mark.

The babies in the hospital—two question marks.

He reviewed the list in his head and decided that five out of the seven could be traced directly back to the antineutrino-*antitrimuon* theory. Of the Telluric Faith he was less certain—unless it was possible that the radiation had affected the townspeople and made them behave in such a bizarre fashion.

And why the babies should *emit* radiation completely baffled him. True, it was only a small amount, not enough to be harmful either to themselves or to anyone who came into contact with them, but why should they be affected in this way at all? Some children had been born perfectly normal while others exhibited this strange behavior pattern. Why? Was it accidental, a random side effect of the radiation which had leaked out of the mine and been genetically transferred from the mothers to their offspring?

He had solved one part of the conundrum only to be faced with other, deeper, more complex problems. Amongst them was the disturbing thought that if this was happening in Gypsum it was almost certainly happening elsewhere in the world. There must be other strata whose mineral composition would make them ideal target areas for antineutrino-*antitrimuon* interaction. And if this same phenomenon was taking place on a global scale it gave rise to the chilling possibility that various parts of the Earth's surface were being subjected to a form of intense interstellar radiation that was affecting the genetic structure of newborn babies.

Frank lit another cigarette and tried hard to recall all that he knew about anti-matter and its place in the

Universe. Of course particles of anti-matter were by no means a new phenomenon—they had been detected many years ago and their physical reality validated by countless experiments. Some scientists believed anti-matter to be comparatively rare in the Universe, and it was indeed true that observation showed the abundance of matter to far outweigh its anti-matter equivalent. But there was another theory that everything in nature was finely balanced—left-hand and right-hand, action and reaction, positive and negative, plus value and minus value—and some argued that if the balance were to be maintained it was only logical to suppose that for every particle of matter there was an equivalent particle of anti-matter.

In other words, there had to exist an Anti-Matter Universe.

Presumably in such a place everything would be reversed: the Anti-Matter Sun would produce antineutrinos instead of neutrinos, natural radioactivity would produce neutrinos instead of antineutrinos. The status quo would be maintained. But what if—as now seemed to be happening—there was a spectacular increase in anti-matter and rather than being a rare occurrence in the Universe particles of anti-matter were challenging particles of matter for supremacy? It was rather a dramatic way in which to view the situation, almost as if the Anti-Matter Universe were seeking to overcome the Universe as it presently existed. But the fact had to be faced that Friedmann's experiments had detected a vastly increased emission of anti-matter from the region of Sagittarius A in the heart of the Milky Way Galaxy, and if such results were found to be true it could only mean that the

Universe and the Anti-Matter Universe were in the throes of some colossal cosmic confrontation.

Was it accidental, Frank wondered, the forces of nature (and presumably anti-nature) locked in a blind meaningless struggle for dominance, the law of survival enacted on a super-galactic scale? Or was there somewhere in the cosmos an Intelligence controlling and directing the influx of anti-matter into the Universe, following a plan that was so vast and incredibly complex as to be beyond the conception of the species of life which crawled upon the face of the Earth?

. . . and of every creeping thing that creepeth upon the earth.

Frank recalled the Biblical phrase quoted by Cabel. It now seemed that the preacher—without knowing it—had stumbled on something approaching the truth: he had founded a religion which believed the Mount of the Holy Cross to be alive, which saw the Earth as a sentient being, and in the sense that deep within the mountain nuclear interactions were taking place he was correct in his belief. The mountain *was* alive in that it was generating vast amounts of radiation. The Earth itself was receiving particles of anti-matter from the center of the Galaxy which were affecting and changing its geophysical structure? Cabel's religious inspiration could be verified and upheld by hard scientific fact.

The waitress removed the untouched meal, shaking her head at the waste and the weird habits of some of the customers. Frank awoke from his reveries and for no sensible reason looked at his watch. He had the feeling that time was pressing, that he ought to be doing something, taking some sort of action, but

166

what action could he take? If his reasoning was correct and his conclusions valid, what could he or anyone do to change things?

It came to him, like a sudden wrench in the heart, that he was the only one in possession of all the facts. Fred Lockyer had one piece of the jigsaw concerning the antineutrino-*antitrimuon* interaction, and Professor Friedmann had the data pertaining to the increase in antineutrinos emanating from the galactic center; but only Frank Kersh knew how the two sets of information related to each other. He was the link between them, possibly the only living person who had so far managed to piece together a series of apparently unconnected events—the latest observational findings on antineutrinos, and current theoretical thinking on the nature of matter/anti-matter particle interaction.

Perhaps the chain of reasoning was faulty in some respect? Couldn't it be argued that Fred Lockyer's speculative assumptions were based not on proven experimental evidence but on abstract theory? High energy physicists were not infallible godlike creatures; they had been known to make false predictions in the past and it was well within the bounds of probability that once again they were trying to theoretically run before they could experimentally walk. It was a faint hope, but the only glimmer of light that Frank could see. He himself wasn't capable of working through Fred Lockyer's hypothesis, of checking it out in step-by-step detail in order to confirm or deny its validity; only an experienced theoretician could do that.

And what if he was correct? What if it were true that at the center of the Galaxy, in the region of Sagittarius A, a new and unknown and incredibly powerful source of energy was beaming particles of anti-matter toward the Earth which would interact to produce high-level radiation?

The question in Frank Kersh's mind was not to ask if and how this were possible: the question was, in heaven's name why?

CHAPTER SEVEN

Cal Renfield was putting the paper to bed, crooning and cursing over it alternately as he came across a piece he liked followed by an item which met with his displeasure. He was stooping over the large oval desk, his shirt sleeves rolled back to reveal freckled, almost hairless arms, reaching without looking for a cigarette which smoldered in the ashtray.

Helen was at the back of the office, mounting photographs on sections of card, the rich red tint of her hair in severe contrast to the pale delicacy of her features, the fine cheekbones and calm grey eyes. She glanced up as Frank came in but carried on with her work, her movements methodical and practiced, swift and yet unhurried. She said without looking up:

"The staff of the *Roaring Fork Bulletin* swings into action to produce yet another issue packed with hard-hitting facts and shattering exposes which lift the lid off the vice and corruption rampant amongst Gypsum's business and political elite. Whose head will roll tomorrow? Which highly-placed politician will pick up his morning paper with trembling hands and see his doom written in the stark black headlines?"

169

"It's a nasty business," Frank said.

"What is?" Cal Renfield inquired absently.

"Packing horse manure into plastic bags."

Cal Renfield grunted, his pencil moving at speed down the copy, initialling each page and racing on to the next.

Helen brought a stack of mounted photographs to the desk, sorted them into the correct order and marked each one with a felt-tip pen. She said, "How about that—my five-legged calf gets the front page spot. When you make it in this town you *really* make it."

"What's your lead story?" Frank asked her.

"Whether or not the local clinic should provide free contraceptive devices for everyone over the age of twenty-one."

"Married or unmarried?"

"Certainly, why not?" Helen said.

"I thought you didn't believe in sex before marriage?"

"Only if it delays the ceremony."

"You two ought to get together as a double-act," Cal Renfield said. "See how many old gags you can get through in half an hour."

"We've been considering that," Helen said, making large goo-goo eyes at Frank in the manner of starlet offering herself to a producer. "Things keep on getting in the way, such as earthquakes, for instance."

Cal Renfield straightened up and blew out his cheeks, signifying that in his opinion he'd done enough work for one day. He threw down the pencil and said, "The sun isn't below the horizon but I feel like a shot of something that'll take the fur off my tongue."

"And the enamel off your teeth," Helen said.

"Anyone care to join me?"

"What about the paper? Is it ready to go to press?" Frank asked.

Cal Renfield nodded and reached for his jacket. "Printer calls for the material at seven. We don't have a press in Gypsum, it's printed in Glenwood Springs. Twenty-seven thousand circulation," he said proudly. "That isn't bad for this neck of the woods."

"I could use a drink myself," Frank said, touching the side of his head.

"Does it still hurt?" Helen said.

Cal Renfield laughed. "Say, that's right, you got biffed this morning by the mad scientist. Started foaming at the mouth, didn't he?" He was smiling broadly, his pug-nosed face squashed into horizontal creases.

"It was a hoot," Frank agreed. "I enjoy getting punched in the stomach occasionally and having my brains rattled. Keeps me in shape and stops me thinking too much."

His expression, or perhaps it was his tone of voice, prompted Helen to say, "Is anything the matter? Were you really hurt this morning?"

"It isn't that."

"What is it then?"

"Let's get that drink first."

She said, becoming concerned, "What is it, Frank? What's happened? Have you heard something from the Project?"

"I received a cable today." Frank took it from the pocket of his leather jacket. "It's from a friend of mine who lectures in high energy physics at the University of Illinois. There's not much point in you reading it because you probably wouldn't understand it."

"Go on," Cal Renfield said, his face now composed, his small grey eyes watchful. "What does it say?"

"I think I'd rather tell you over a drink."

"If it's that serious it looks like we're going to need one," Helen said.

She turned and went to the door, holding it open as Frank and Cal Renfield followed her. They were about to go out when the phone rang.

"Shit," Cal Renfield numbled. He hesitated, in two minds, and said, "The hell with it. I've had enough for one day."

Helen said, "You'd better answer it, it could be the *Washington Post* asking for me."

Cal Renfield muttered another obscenity and trudged across the office. He picked the receiver up, said "*Bulletin,*" and after a moment, "Yeah," and held the receiver out. "It's for you."

Frank took it from him, a dull feeling of unease gathering in his stomach. He didn't know what to expect but the sense of foreboding warned him that the call was going to be neither social nor pleasant.

It was Lee Merriam, who said immediately, "Thank Christ I've found you. I've been trying to reach you for over an hour. Can you get up here right away?"

"What is it? What's wrong?"

"We've found Professor Friedmann. That's to say we know where he is but we can't get to him."

"Where is he?"

"In the detection chamber. But we can't get through."

"Why not?"

There was a slight though perceptible pause.

"I don't know, Frank, I can't figure it out. I sent a party of six down—" He broke off as if in anger or frustration, his breathing heavy on the line. "They couldn't get to him. They said there was a blockage in the main tunnel, some kind of obstacle. I don't know what the hell they're on about."

"You mean a rockfall?" Frank said.

"No, not a rockfall. They said it was a . . . blank wall blocking the tunnel. A solid blank wall of black rock. I mean, what the hell can that be?"

"I don't know," Frank said. "I'll be right with you."

He put the phone down.

Part Three

THE FLOOD

CHAPTER ONE

Lee Merriam met them in the compound. His square rugged face was impassive, the diagonal scar on his forehead like a pale brand against the dark leathery texture of his skin. He didn't say anything but led the way into the hut and shut the door carefully behind them; Frank noticed that the drawers of the filing cabinet were hanging open and all the contents removed. The computer print-out was also missing.

"Do they know what's happened?" Lee Merriam said, referring to Cal Renfield and his daughter.

"I told them what you told me on the phone."

"What do you make of it?"

"It could be a rockfall."

"That's no rockfall," Lee Merriam said emphatically. "The guys I sent down are experienced engineers who know this mine pretty good. If it had been a rockfall they would have said so. The main tunnel is completely blocked—" he held up the palms of both hands and swept them sideways "—just a smooth blank slab of rock that looks as if it's been sliced by a razor. Now you tell me what that is and where it came from."

175

"And Professor Friedmann is on the other side of it?"

"Right," said Lee Merriam, nodding.

"Is anyone with him?"

"Not that we know of. There's nobody missing, so presumably he's alone."

"How do you know he's down there?"

"I spoke to him," Lee Merriam said, glancing warily at Cal Renfield as if he might be giving too much away. The look in his eyes was one Frank had difficulty in reading: guarded and unsure. He went on, "I had somebody keep trying to reach him and eventually he came on the line. Couldn't get a lick of sense out of him. I was about to ask what was happening down there when the line went dead—anyways he put the phone down, or something happened—and since then I haven't been able to make contact."

"You're convinced it was Professor Friedmann?"

"It was the Professor. No mistake," Lee Merriam said with heavy finality.

"What did he say, when you spoke to him?" Cal Renfield asked, hitching up his trouser leg and easing himself onto the corner of the desk.

"He just babbled on, I couldn't make sense of it."

"But what actually did he say?" asked Frank.

Lee Merriam stared at the floor for a moment, either trying to remember or pretending to have forgotten. Then he sighed and gave a slight shrug of his burly shoulders. "He said something about 'the Earth will cast them out and seal up its secret places,' whatever that means. And he kept going on about 'waters from heaven' and 'the breath of life' and stuff like that. Look, I told you, it didn't make any sense.

176

The man was obviously disturbed, he didn't know what he was saying—"

"The preacher," Helen said.

"What?" Lee Merriam said sharply.

"Those are the words the preacher, Cabel, uses. His sermons are full of phrases like that. Has Professor Friedmann ever heard him preach?"

"How the hell should I know?" Lee Merriam said irritably, flexing his arms and swinging them. He was a large physical man who sought to use his strength to overcome problems, and now he felt bound, frustrated, unable to act positively.

Frank said, "Maybe Professor Friedmann has been converted to the Telluric Faith and taken Cabel's preaching to heart: he's sealed off the mountain according to instructions." He was smiling gently, not entirely serious, just wondering if the sound of it carried any credence.

"And what happens next?" Cal Renfield said sardonically. "Flood waters from heaven? Bolts of lightning from the blue?"

"That's the twenty-four-billion-dollar question," Frank said. "What does happen next?"

"What happens next is that we get him out of there," Lee Merriam said grimly.

"How do you propose to do that?" Frank said.

"That's why I called you. Last time you found a way through into the detection chamber by another route. If you did it once you should be able to do it again. Can you remember how you managed to get through?" His blue eyes watched Frank keenly, anxious for an affirmative response.

Frank nibbled his lower lip. "I'm not sure," he said

slowly, careful not to look at anyone. "In any case, wasn't the tunnel blocked by the tremor after I'd gone through? One of your men reported that the roof caved in."

"We could clear it, dig a way through," Lee Merriam said. He looked at Frank urgently. "At least it's worth a try. There's no other way to get to him. It's the only chance we've got."

"Couldn't you break through the rock that's blocking the main tunnel?" Cal Renfield asked.

Lee Merriam gave a sour smile that was more like a grimace. "We already tried that."

"What happened?"

"Nothing—except we broke three drills."

"Explosives?" Helen said tentatively.

"And bring the mountain down on top of us?" Lee Merriam said. He shook his head vigorously. "There's only one way to get through into the detection chamber and it's the way Frank went in the first time. Otherwise Professor Friedmann is sealed in good and tight, like a mouse in a granite tomb. There's no other way to reach him."

Helen said, "Come on, Frank, you've got to remember. Christ, it was only three days ago."

"That's right," Frank said. "And a lot can happen in three days."

Helen threw up her hands in mock despair. "This country's leading science writer," she told Lee Merriam, "and he can't even remember where he stashed the loot."

"Listen," Lee Merriam said, trying to be decisive. "We can get as far as the blocked tunnel, right? One of the guys who went with you the first time can get us that far. We clear the rubble away and put in fresh supports—then you take over and lead us through. If it's that complicated to remember right now maybe it'll come back to you when we're actually down there."

"Maybe," Frank said non-committally.

"You don't sound too thrilled with the idea," Cal Renfield said. He had been watching Frank closely.

"To tell the truth, I'm not, because I don't think it'll work. It was pure fluke that I found a way through last time, a freak accident you might almost call it. I don't think it's going to happen twice."

"So you're not even prepared to try?" Lee Merriam said. His face had grown sullen, disappointed.

"There has to be another way." Frank shook his head hopelessly and happened to glance at the empty filing cabinet. "What have you done with the files? And the printout?"

"I've got three of the technical personnel going through them piece by piece," Lee Merriam answered. "It might just be that there's something which can tell us what that black rock is and what it's doing there. Professor Friedmann might have known all along of a way to seal the main tunnel—maybe he had it installed before the Project got started."

"*Installed?*" Frank said. He grinned incredulously. "You think the black rock is an artifact, that it was manufactured and placed in position by a team of engineers?"

"It's possible."

"I don't think so."

"For somebody who's never seen it you sound mighty positive of that fact."

179

Frank hesitated. He was about to tell them and then something made him decide not to. Why shouldn't they know? What was he afraid of, ridicule? No, it was something deeper than that, something more serious that he himself hadn't yet fathomed. And in a sense he was relieved that the existence of the black rock had been confirmed by independent witnesses; for he had to admit that it had crossed his mine more than once that what he had seen and experienced was nothing more substantial than a hallucinatory vision, the imaginary product of a mind which had become confused and frightened. But now he knew differently. The black rock was a geophysical reality, embedded a mile underground in the depths of the Telluride Mine.

He said smoothly, "I don't think it could have been installed for the simple reason that it isn't shown on any of the plans and diagrams. Come on, Lee, the two of us looked over those in close detail, remember? A construction like that would be marked."

"It would be," Lee Merriam agreed, "unless Professor Friedmann wanted it kept secret."

"For what reason?"

"Hell, how do I know? The way he's been behaving it'd take a genius or a madman to understand his motivation. All I know is that somehow or other we've got to get through to the detection chamber. How we're going to do it I don't know, but we've got to try."

Frank became still for a moment. A thought had lit up in his mind like an electric light illuminating a pitch-black cellar. He turned to Lee Merriam and said, "We've overlooked one vital factor in all this."

"What's that?"

"Why are we all sitting around trying to figure out what Professor Friedmann is doing down there and how we can reach him when Karl Leach is obviously the man we should be talking to? It might even be that Leach knows how to get past the black rock and into the detection chamber. He was in charge of the underground installation; if anyone knows what Professor Friedmann is up to it should be him."

Lee Merriam didn't immediately seize upon this brilliant notion.

"Well?" Frank demanded.

"I'm afraid Dr. Leach isn't in any fit state to advise anybody about anything," Lee Merriam said soberly.

"What do you mean?"

"After you left this morning we had to put him under heavy sedation. I thought his condition was temporary, that he was overwrought and just needed to calm down and take it easy for a while. Seems I was mistaken."

"What happened?" asked Cal Renfield.

"What didn't happen, you mean. He came around and clobbered Smitty—that's the medical orderly—with a chair. Damn near broke his neck. Then he starts running all over the place yelling at the top of his voice. He even tried to go underground but we stopped him just in time. He's only a little guy but you wouldn't believe the strength of the man—took three of us to restrain him and get him quieted down again."

"We believe you," Helen said.

"Where is he now?" Frank said.

"In the sick bay."

"Sedated?"

"No," said Lee Merriam heavily. "Strapped down. And that's how he stays till we get a doctor to look him over. I'm taking no more chances."

"With Professor Friedmann underground and Dr. Leach on the surface, seems like you got your hands full," Cal Renfield said, lighting a cigarette. He gave the impression of being ironically amused by it all, rather as if this was only what he had been expecting —and now that his prediction had come true he could view the situation with a kind of indulgent mockery. Frank recognized this as the trait that Helen had inherited, the same rather cynical world-weary attitude toward the passing parade with its follies and false hopes and foolish vanities.

"I'd like to see him," Frank said.

"It won't do any good," Lee Merriam insisted. "I tried to talk to him earlier. He wasn't making any sense."

"Just the same, Lee."

Lee Merriam sighed, shaking his head as if granting a favor under sufferance, and without a word led them to another hut where they found the medical orderly, his head swathed in bandages, keeping an uneasy watch over the patient. Dr. Leach was strapped to a leather couch, eyes closed, black hair awry; he appeared to be asleep.

"He hasn't moved for the past hour," Smitty reported. He glanced suspiciously at the supine man on the bench. "But after what happened last time I wouldn't expect that to mean a thing. The guy is deranged. Absolutely."

Frank remembered the medical orderly as the nervous young man who hadn't wished to be left alone when the rescue party had been checking out the tunnels. Now he looked particularly woebegone, and with a rapid uneasy flicker in his eyes as if half-expecting Dr. Leach to suddenly break free and make a leap for his throat with clawed hands.

"You haven't given him a shot of anything?" Frank said.

The young man shook his head. "I don't want to go anywhere near him. Just send for the doctor and ship him out of here." He stood well away from the bench, keeping a clear distance.

"We're wasting time," Lee Merriam said impatiently. "Come on, Frank, this isn't going to do any good. The guy is off his head, he isn't going to be of any help to us now."

"Are you hoping he might tell us something?" Helen asked.

"He know's Professor Friedmann better than anybody, so it's possible he knows why the Professor has gone down into the detection chamber and the reason he's sealed himself in—if that, in fact, is what's happened." He looked at Lee Merriam. "It could be that Professor Friedmann is being held there against his will."

"Held there?" Lee Merriam said, frowning. "But there's nobody else in the mine. What are you talking about?"

Frank went over to the bench and Dr. Leach's eyes opened instantly. They were wild and dark. The thick unbroken growth of his eyebrows was like a black bar across his forehead. He stared at Frank without recognition, lying perfectly still, and it was Helen who voiced the thought that was in Frank's mind.

"He looks exactly like one of the babies," she said wonderingly, her tone perplexed. "The kids in the hospital—don't you think so?" she appealed to her father.

"I wouldn't have said so," Cal Renfield replied pragmatically.

Frank stood at the side of the bench, gazing calmly down on Dr. Leach; he could almost feel the tension in the small strongly-built body, the nervous and emotional energy surging through him like electricity. Had his brain, as those of the four scientists, also been affected by radiation? Was there a tiny malevolent tumor slowly unfolding behind those wild staring eyes, infiltrating the health brain cells and replacing them with the poison of madness, the ultimate finality of death?

He said quietly, "Why did you want to go underground, Karl? Were you trying to help Professor Friedmann?

Dr. Leach blinked twice, very slowly, like somebody who has just awakened in a strange room and can't remember how he came to be there. It crossed Frank's mind that perhaps he had lost the power of speech, that he had been struck dumb, and he was therefore surprised by the sane, reasonable tone of Leach's voice as if he were carrying on a normal conversation that had been momentarily interrupted.

"It was Edmund who first had the idea, I admit that. He told me and I didn't believe him. Would you have believed him? Would anybody? He had to prove it to me—I insisted on that—and he did prove it. The count was high, we expected that. It only confirmed what we already knew. But I will admit, I am perfectly willing to admit, that it was Edmund who first had the idea. And he proved it."

He smiled quite gently, almost dreamily, as if at a fond recollection.

"Was it the count that proved it to you?" Frank asked in the same conversational tone.

"No, no . . ." Leach shook his head, experiencing difficulty due to the tightness of the leather straps binding his arms and chest. There was a stubble of beard on his jaw through which gleamed a faint sheen of perspiration. "I told you, weren't you listening? We already *knew*—Edmund knew and he proved it to me. The count merely confirmed it. A rate of 3×10^4—it was very exciting when the print-out confirmed it. We had a little celebration, Edmund and I, because then we knew we were right."

"Right about the antineutrinos," Frank said.

"*No,*" said Karl Leach snappily, in the manner of someone being willfully misunderstood. "The increased rate of antineutrinos only served to prove that we had been right all along. That Edmund's theory was validated."

"So the count finally confirmed it; but how did Edmund prove it to you in the first place? What did he say to convince you?"

"He proved it to me. I've already said that. He proved it to me."

"Yes, but how?"

Leach stared blankly past Frank's head, his eyes fixed on the ceiling; they became glazed and lost; was he entering into a coma or simply trying to remember?

"How did he prove his theory?" Frank persisted

softly. "His theory of—?"

"His theory about the Earth." Leach came back to himself. "His theory about the Earth five billion years ago."

Frank breathed slowly and carefully. "Before it was formed."

"His theory about the plasma in space. The plasma drifted in space, it was conscious, possessed intelligence, had the power of logical thought."

"And the plasma became the Earth. The plasma that was conscious coalesced to form the Earth—is that what Edmund believed?"

"For ten billion years, since the instant of Creation, the plasma had evolved, drifting in space, seeking form and identity. Edmund knew that. He knew that one day it would find form and identity and become the Sun and the planets. He was proved right, it came to pass, the Sun and the planets were formed. We are the living proof' that Edmund was right."

Karl Leach had begun to tense against the straps, his fists clenching and opening, clenching again. His dark eyes were fierce, staring into space, lost in mysterious visions.

"Edmund was proved right," Frank prompted him. He wanted Leach to continue his line of thought, yet he seemed to be drifting away, inhabiting another plane of existence.

"Yes," said Leach in a curious drone.

"The Sun and the planets were formed from the plasma which had drifted in space since the beginning of Creation. Edmund believed that and he proved it to you—"

"But the Earth had waited. It had waited five billion years to be awakened. It had lain dormant, sleeping, awaiting the signal. That was when we knew that the Earth was ready to awaken. Its consciousness was to be awakened for the first time in five billion years."

Frank waited a moment, studying the malformed human being who was twisting and turning against the straps. The sweat from his chest and armpits had spread like a dark stain across the front of his shirt.

"The signal," Frank said quietly."The signal came to the Earth in the form of antineutrinos."

"The rate was 3×10^4," said Karl Leach with great satisfaction. "We knew it would come. It was only a matter of time. Edmund had said it would come *in our lifetime.*" He sounded exultant.

"And then you knew he was right."

"The signal came. It came in our lifetime."

"Edmund was proved right."

"Yes," said Leach, hissing it.

"Why has he gone below?" Frank asked casually, slipping the question in as if it were only of minor interest.

"To prepare the way," Leach said, the obvious answer to a naive question.

"Yes of course," Frank said. "To prepare the way." He glanced sideways at the others, who had become immobile; the medical orderly had retreated even further, standing behind Lee Merriam in an attempt to put as much muscle and brawn between him and the sweating staring man on the couch.

Helen was about to speak and Frank cautioned her to remain silent. He said in a gentle, agreeable tone, "Does Edmund need your help, Karl? Or can he prepare the way alone?"

"Edmund is the leader. He will make the path straight. The signal will come, bringing the Message from the center of the Galaxy. Edmund awaits the Message and then everything will be made known: he has prepared the way: everything is ready."

"And what is the message? Does Edmund know? Do you know?"

"When it comes all will be made known. The Earth will awaken, it will become conscious and sentient once more. It has slept in silence for five billion years and now the way has been prepared. The signal comes, the Message is received, the Earth will awaken . . . "

His eyes became sightless, gazing beyond the confines of the room with a dull fixedness as if witnessing cosmic events out there in the depths of space. He had ceased to live in the real world: his surroundings were no more than vague shadows, the people insubstantial phantoms flitting on the edge of his conscious awareness. Reality for Dr. Karl Leach comprised the stream of antineutrinos flooding in from the galactic center at the speed of light. With them they brought information which would trigger the awakening of the planet. It was all there, taking place in front of his eyes, his head filled with wondrous visions of the Earth regaining consciousness after five billion years.

Frank realized that Leach was reaching a stage when he would either lapse into a coma or become totally incoherent, losing altogether the facility to communicate. The vital question was did he know how to get through into the detection chamber? Was there some way to get past the black rock and reach Professor Friedmann before he was able to carry out the preparation for . . . what? How was he to "make the path straight," as Leach called it? Did it involve the detection tanks—or was it more a mental preparation, a kind of metaphysical rite that Professor Friedmann had to perform?

Frank had to repeat Leach's name several times before his eyes hardened into focus. The thick black hair was wet at the roots, strands of it clinging to his neck and forehead.

"We want to help Edmund," Frank said in a soft urgent whisper. "We want to help him prepare the way. Listen, Karl, how do we help him? You must tell us how to reach him."

"No longer possible. The mountain will not allow it. The Earth has sealed up its secret places. Too late."

Again a phrase that was reminiscent of Cabel's preaching: the belief in the mountain as a living organism, a conscious terrestial force that had the inherent dynamism to alter its geophysical structure.

"There must be a way through, Karl."

"No way possible. The chamber is sealed. Edmund must prepare the way. The mountain will protect him."

"How must he prepare? What has he to do?"

Leach smiled glassily, a sly child harboring a secret.

"Is it something to do with the tanks? Does he need to change the chemical balance to speed up the rate of interaction?"

Karl Leach continued to smile. His face was an empty smiling mask concealing a hundred thousand million brain cells engaged in civil war. If the signal came and the Message was received and the Earth awakened it was unlikely he would ever know about it.

They were standing in the compound looking toward the bright orange fretwork above the mine-head which supported the winding gear. Lee Merriam said, "Do you believe me now? Didn't I tell you that Dr. Leach is off his rocker?"

"Maybe less than we suppose," Frank said.

"Come on now," Lee Merriam protested. "All this stuff about the Earth coming alive—you can't seriously believe that a signal from outer space is going to awaken it after five billion years."

"Professor Friedmann obviously believes it to be true."

"And do you?" Helen said.

"I don't know. It's a fact that the Earth is being bombarded by a vastly increased flood of antineutrinos from the galactic center. The latest theory suggests that these are interacting with other particles and producing large amounts of radiation. In that sense the mountain is coming alive. The thing I can't understand is what Professor Friedmann has to do to prepare the way—why is he down there at all, sealed in the detection chamber?"

"You mean being protected by the mountain, don't you?" Helen said, raising her eyebrows sardonically.

"We shouldn't just dismiss what we can't understand," Frank told her. "I agree that Leach's story sounds incredible but you have to admit that it answers a lot of the questions about what's been happening in this area lately. How else can you explain the freak weather conditions, the earth tremors, the strange way people have been behaving?"

"And the babies," Helen said. "Don't forget them."

"I hadn't forgotten," Frank said. "If you want to know, that's the one thing that bothers me most of all. Because if it's happening here in Gypsum it's likely to be happening elsewhere at the same time."

"You mean elsewhere in the States?" Cal Renfield said.

"And throughout the world. Wherever the geophysical strata are similar to what we have here in the mountain—tellurous ore—then it's possible that the same phenomena are taking place."

Lee Merriam said bluntly, "What concerns me is the here and now." He looked searchingly at Frank. "If there's no way past the black rock we'll have to try and reach him via the upper level, and you're the only one who knows how to get through."

"That's what I like about you, Lee. You're so subtle."

"Are you prepared to make the attempt?"

"Do I have a choice?"

Cal Renfield said, "Listen, I don't understand any of this scientific stuff about particles and interactions; what I'd like to know is what damage can Friedmann do down there? If the guy really is nutty could he do something to the equipment in the detection chamber, maybe cause an explosion?" His soft round features were molded into an expression that was both inquiring and concerned.

Frank shook his head, an admission that he wasn't sure. He said, "There's radiation equipment down there for detecting the presence of argon-37. Ordinarily there's no danger because it's shielded, and in any case the amount of radiation is quite small. But if the particle interactions have been building up in the tanks and the radiation level is high . . . "

"Then what could Friedmann do?" Cal Renfield asked.

"Basically, one of two things. He could either allow the radiation level to escalate to a point where it became unstable—and then you would indeed get an explosion. Or he could release it."

"You mean let the radiation just leak out?"

"That's right. Possibly it wouldn't do much damage because it's a mile underground—it would be dissipated through the tunnels. Anybody down there, of course, wouldn't stand much of a chance."

"Including Friedmann?" Cal Renfield said.

Frank nodded.

"And anybody who went down to get him out of there," Helen said, not looking at anyone. She gazed toward the winding gear in its steel framework.

Lee Merriam glanced at his watch. He was impatient for action. "We can be kitted out and ready to go in ten minutes. If it's a major fall we'll need pickaxes and shoring material. Ideally we could use two parties, the first to clear away the rubble, the second to follow on afterward. The first party could act as a back-up if the main rescue team runs into trouble. Say eight men in two teams of four. I'll get the first team off right away and they can be making a start on the clearing operation. We'll give them thirty minutes to make some kind of headway and then follow them down."

Lee Merriam was happy to be planning and organizing and getting ready to move; this was positive action, not abstract scientific speculation. He couldn't get a grip on theories, they were too diffuse, too elusive.

While he went to get things started Frank told Cal Renfield and Helen about the cable, explaining in more detail Fred Lockyer's hypothesis of antineutrino-*antitrimuon* interactions. They listened blankly, hardly understanding a word, though he took pains to make it as simple and straightforward as possible.

When he had finished, Cal Renfield said incredulously, "You mean to say that the Telluric Faith might really be on to something? That Cabel isn't just spouting a load of religious bullshit?"

"In an odd way he could be right. Cabel's beliefs, Professor Friedmann's research data and Fred Lockyer's theory all seem to point to the same kind of phenomenon—yet they each approach it in a different way and describe it in their own terms. It isn't the first time that religion, cosmology and high energy physics have found themselves to be bedfellows. Though pretty uneasy ones, I grant you."

"But surely Karl Leach was raving when he talked about the Earth being formed out of—what did he call it?—conscious plasma? The Earth is inanimate, it isn't alive."

"Not in the sense that we understand it," Frank agreed. "But our knowledge of life forms in the Universe is limited to those on this planet. It'd be rather arrogant of the human race to claim to be the only type of life form extant in all of Creation. Maybe there is such a thing as "conscious plasma" which lives in space. We simply don't know. I doubt whether Fred Lockyer would dismiss the idea out of hand. He'd keep an open mind until he came up with evidence which either proved or denied its existence."

"And I thought physics was all to do with rubbing fur on an ebonite rod," Helen said, looking as bemused as a child on its first day at school.

"In your case that has more to do with Freudian symbolism," Frank said, grinning. "What you choose to do in your leisure time is your own affair."

She pouted and gave him a smoldering look. "You'd better make sure you come back out of that mine, Frank Kersh. We still have an account to settle."

They watched the first team of four men heading for the cage. Lee Merriam saw them away and then came across the compound. He glanced up at the sky, which was darkening as the late afternoon ebbed into evening. The sky was clear, with just a few wisps of nimbus to the east, and already the first faint stars were winking on overhead. It looked as though it was going to be a calm peaceful night.

"We follow them down in one hour," said Lee Merriam crisply. He almost seemed to be enjoying himself. "This time I'm coming with you."

"That sounds like you don't trust me."

"If there's a way through into the detection chamber I want to know about it. And I want to be there when we reach Professor Friedmann."

"If we reach him," Frank said, sounding a note of caution. "I told you, Lee, I'm not at all sure I can find my way through like I did last time. It was pretty confusing after the tremor, you know."

Why didn't he tell them? Why not come right out with it and say that something had happened in the depths of the Telluride Mine which defied rational explanation and flouted all the rules of normal physical behavior? Why was he so reluctant to admit to anyone that he had witnessed—had actually been part of—a strange occurrence which had someone recounted it to him he would have scoffed at and probably laughed in their face? Was he too afraid of their scepticism and pitying glances?

The truth was (and he was only just beginning to realize and accept it) that it had shaken the very foundation of his absolute certitude in scientific method and procedure. The experience had been subjective, inexplicable, and utterly mystifying—none of which were satisfactory criteria in the strict scientific sense—and yet he believed in the validity of it, knew without any doubt that it had actually taken place. How was he to reconcile his rational, objective outlook with the emotional and intuitive part of his nature which accepted the experience for no other reason than that it had happened? His normal response would have been to reject it out of hand.

The difference, of course, was that this time it had happened to him.

Helen was in the act of lighting a cigarette when they felt it; the lighter flame hovered an inch from the cigarette and her eyes came up to meet Frank's.

A deep and distant and unmistakable tremor.

"That's all we need," said Lee Merriam, almost angrily.

"Might have been an explosion," Cal Renfield suggested.

Helen rolled her eyes melodramatically and said, "No, it was the Earth waking up. You know, early alarm call."

"I like your sense of humor," Frank said. "You should have been an undertaker."

But the vibration had been so faint that a moment later they all wondered if they had imagined it. The evening was gentle and unruffled, the dusk gradually encroaching like a soft blue mist, quite unperturbed by the events happening deep in the Earth's core. The stars were coming on one by one.

CHAPTER THREE

Even as a child he had never been afraid of the dark. He had never slept with the light on and the threat of bogie-men coming to get him during the night had always seemed, even then, to lack menace and credibility. But the darkness within the mountain was a palpable thing, dense and claustrophobic; it filled the tunnels with black air that pressed against his face with a chilly dampness and entered his mouth like the taste of old rusty iron.

The foul stagnant smell reminded him of animal matter slowly decomposing, and it was with an effort that he tried to dismiss from his mind the image of the four of them as tiny microbes in the intestines of a large cold-blooded creature: the endless labyrinth of tunnels forming an enclosed system, leading nowhere, without entrances and exits.

The first team had partially cleared away the debris and had done the best they could to shore up the tunnel with odd pieces of timber which littered the workings. In the light of the lamps it looked none too safe and Frank voiced the opinion that a decent sneeze would bring the whole assembly down on top of them.

"How much more do you reckon there is to move?" Lee Merriam asked one of his engineers.

"It's not as bad as it looks," the man answered, annoyed by Frank's comment and letting him see it. "The tunnel narrows beyond this point and the roof seems to have held. If we clear the entrance you should be able to get through without any problems."

"Famous last words," Frank said drily.

"You try digging it out with your bare hands," the engineer came back at him hotly. "We've no powered equipment, no proper lighting—"

"Okay, okay, boys," Lee Merriam said placatingly. "This is difficult enough without squabbling; let's all just do the best we can and leave it at that."

He went forward to inspect how the work was progressing, his large beefy face grim and determined in the light from the heavy-duty lamps. It suddenly occurred to Frank that Lee Merriam was so desperately keen to find a way through into the detection chamber that he wondered whether it was from a sense of duty or if there was an ulterior motive. Of course he was only doing his job, yet even so his anxiety seemed to be verging on the obsessional.

He came back and reported that it was almost clear, except for one or two boulders that were too big to be moved. "We'll have to squeeze past those," he said, sucking in his stomach. "This is when I could do to be carrying thirty pounds less weight. The tunnel looks in reasonable condition from there on in—as far as we can see, anyway. Can you remember what it's like further on? Do we keep to this tunnel or cut off into another?"

"We keep to this one. It gets pretty narrow further on."

"You do remember some of it," Lee Merriam said. He watched Frank's face intently in the dim light.

"Some," Frank conceded.

"There must be one helluva gradient if it drops to the level of the chamber."

"That's the part I can't recall. We'll come to some old workings and there's a large main tunnel leading off it the other side. From there we'll have to take it as it comes."

"That tremor must have really shook you up."

Frank didn't reply. He looked to where the men were clearing the last of the rubble, partly obscured by dust which swirled in the beams of the lamps.

"We're about set to go," Lee Merriam said. "Do you want me to lead the way?"

"No, I'll go first. There's a chance it'll come back to me if I recognize any of the features." He smiled inwardly, thinking that he would recognize the mirror-like black rock soon enough if he ever set eyes on it again. But he didn't expect the rock to be at the end of the tunnel as before: it had moved to the lower level, hadn't it? Assuming there was only one mysterious black rock in the Telluride Mine.

The engineer in charge of the clearing operation called out that it was now clear enough to proceed and added caustically that he hoped no one would sneeze as they went through.

The tunnel was as familiar to Frank as the recurrence of a bad dream. Without thinking about it he started counting the number of paces in his head, knowing that by the hundredth the four of them should have reached the small cavern with its shallow workings . . . and beyond that the tunnel where he had seen the reflection of his lamp signalling to him.

Lee Merriam was close behind, his breathing magnified by the confined space, and by an odd trick of the acoustics it seemed to be coming from some distance ahead—preceding them into the depths of the mountain.

Frank suddenly began to exude cold sweat. He thought: This is madness, tempting fate twice. I survived one tremor and got the hell out of the place. What am I doing, repeating the same stupid mistake? The mountain let me off once, it isn't going to be so magnanimous a second time.

And then he thought: I'm getting to be as crazy as Friedmann and Leach and all the others, imagining the mountain to be alive. Next I'll be thinking that it knows we're here inside its entrails, waiting for the moment with sly malice when with a single muscle contraction it will squash us into smears of blood and splinters of bone. Quit it, he told himself. You're surrounded by dead unfeeling inanimate rock. Nothing exists down here, nothing is alive, nothing can pass through solid granite.

Except neutrinos and antineutrinos.

The tunnel narrowed, became lower, just as he remembered. It was gradually descending and bearing to the left. Shortly it would begin to—

In a sudden seizure of panic he thought: What is this, what's happening? *It should be bearing to the right.* Have I got it wrong? Was it to the left or to the right?

And he knew without any doubt that before the tunnel had curved in the opposite direction—which was plainly impossible. How could a man-made tunnel alter its course. The answer was that it couldn't and yet it had.

He stumbled on through the dust, now obliged to bend his head as the roof became lower and the tunnel itself more confined. The beam of the lamp illuminated the smooth concave walls and the steady downward curve to the left: a tube becoming smaller and smaller as it sank deeper into the Earth.

Lee Merriam was breathing strenuously from the exertion of having to walk in such a cramped crouching fashion: it was punishing to the legs and the small of the back. He said, wheezing, "If this gets any narrower you're gonna need a shoehorn to ease me through." Already his shoulders were brushing the sides of the tunnel.

Frank didn't answer. His body moved mechanically forward while he attempted to figure out what could have caused the tunnel's change in direction. There might have been a slippage of the strata, the bedrock shifting as a result of the tremor, but surely the tunnel wouldn't have remained intact? At some point its course would have been disrupted as the vast pressure of rock twisted it out of shape. There had to be another explanation. The trouble was, he couldn't think of one.

They were now having to slant their bodies sideways in order to move along. If the tunnel decreased much more they would have no choice but to halt and retrace their steps. And it was becoming stuffier, the air stale and foul-tasting, which made breathing even more difficult.

"When does it start to open out?" Lee Merriam asked, gasping.

"Any time now," Frank said, wondering if by some bizarre chance they would come upon the cavern and the old workings mysteriously transposed into the mirror-image of themselves, everything reversed in exact detail as in a perfect reflection. Not the true image, but the anti-image.

Was that what had happened? Were the antineutrinos responsible for creating a complete and faithful reproduction *in reverse*? Could they have changed the metabolism of the strata so that it was transformed from matter into antimatter? He was reminded of the antineutrino-*antitrimuon* interaction and wondered if this was one possible side-effect, the nuclear transmutation of particles into their anti-particle equivalents?

The tunnel was now at its narrowest and Lee Merriam was in real difficulty. His progress was slow and labored, moving sideways one step at a time, his body scraping against the walls and in danger of becoming wedged.

He said, "This is no good, Frank. Any minute now I'm going to get stuck good and fast. Can you see up ahead—does it begin to open out? If it doesn't I'll have to go back."

Frank directed the lamp along the narrow fissure and the beam was lost in inky blackness. It touched nothing, illuminated no rock, threw back no reflected light.

"We're almost there. If you can make it through this section it seems to open out; I can't see anything, but I guess it must be a large cavern."

He thought: A large cavern that wasn't there before. Is the mountain playing games with us? Does it know just where we are and what we're doing, laying traps for us, making caverns appear from nowhere, having fun at our expense?

He squeezed through the last few feet and came out of a thin cleft in the rock face and nearly stepped over the edge of a precipice into black space. It wasn't a cavern after all, but a large jagged shaft which went straight down, the sides sheer and vertical dropping away into the depths. The dank sour smell was very strong now, borne up on a draught of chill air.

"Watch your step, Lee. There's nothing here but a narrow ledge about three feet wide. Keep your back to the rock face."

Lee Merriam edged carefully onto the lip of rock, sliding each foot experimentally before trusting it to carry his weight. He was breathing gustily. "You didn't warn us about this, Frank. How do we reach the cavern from here?"

"You tell me. This shaft wasn't here before."

The other two men sidled onto the ledge and one of them said, "Christ, what a stench! Where's it coming from?"

"Down there," Lee Merriam said unnecessarily. "Wasn't this the way you came before?" he asked Frank.

"I'm not sure. Everything's changed." He swept his lamp around, trying to make out the far perimeter of the shaft, but the beam wouldn't reach across what he was only now beginning to realize must be an enormous yawning pit in the heart of the mountain.

"If this wasn't here before it must have been caused

by the tremor. Maybe the whole inside of the mountain fell apart and left this hole. Can't see any other explanation."

"Neither can I," Frank said, but he wasn't happy with Lee Merriam's interpretation. An underground landslide of these proportions would have sent the seismic recorders wild for miles around; it would have registered as a severe turbulence almost on the scale of a major earthquake.

"I guess this is as far as we go," said one of the men. He was trying not to sound relieved but his voice betrayed the fact that he was rather glad they weren't able to proceed any further.

Lee Merriam shone his lamp down into the shaft, which had less effect than a match in a train tunnel. "What do you think? Is there a way to get down?"

"If it's a natural fissure it could be miles deep. And how do we know if it'll take us into the detection chamber or not?"

"I guess you're right. But at least it's going in the right direction," Lee Merriam said with mournful mock humor.

"We don't have the equipment," said one of the other men. "You're gonna need an experienced underground rescue team to get down *that*."

They stood close against the rock face, staring into the fathomless blackness and debating what—if anything—could be done. In the end they all agreed it was a hopeless situation and there was no alternative but to return. Frank didn't care to admit it, but he was more than a little relieved himself. He wanted to get back on the surface before the mountain decided to open up any new chasms right under their feet and

and consign all four of them to the Ultimate Void.

Lee Merriam said reluctantly, "All right, there's not much we can do here. Let's get on back." Frank heard him shuffling sideways in the darkness, feeling cautiously for the narrow cleft in the rock face, and then an irritable exclamation. More scrabbling, followed this time by a couple of genuine obscenities.

"What's the problem?"

"This is stupid. I can't find the entrance to the tunnel. It was here, right here, by my right hand, and now I can't locate it." There were further sounds of him fumbling his way along, and then he encountered the outstretched arm of one of the other men feeling its way toward him. He swung his lamp around to examine the rock face: the cleft had been between the two of them and now it wasn't. The rock was flawed with small cracks but none was wider than the thickness of a finger.

"Hey, Jerry," Lee Merriam said to the man nearest him, "how far along there did you move?"

"We didn't. Frank just moved far enough to let me get on the ledge."

"I did?" Frank said, disconcerted. "I'm over here, on the other side of Lee."

"No, he means me," said the other man.

Frank nodded, thankful to have solved that little puzzle: there were two Franks. But where the hell was the entrance to the tunnel?

The same dull unease rose up in his chest like a faint yet persistent pain. They were being observed: the mountain had altered the direction of the tunnel and deliberately led them to this central pit: now they were here it had sealed off the entrance, leaving them stranded on a rocky ledge with an unimaginable drop directly in front of them. Was it really possible for this to have happened? Of course it wasn't, his mind rejected the thought, mountains weren't able to change their inner structure at will; yet his disbelief didn't alter the fact that the four of them were standing precariously on a narrow ledge in almost total darkness, nor that Lee Merriam was still unable to locate the tunnel entrance, despite the mounting fervor of his language.

The man to his right—Jerry—was tapping hopefully at the rock face with a small pick, as if the right sequence of taps would magically reveal the missing tunnel. Evidently he still believed in fairytales.

Lee Merriam thought it high time he became decisive. "Everybody turn their lamps on the rock. Let's examine every square inch of this son of a bitch. We just came out of that tunnel and it has to be there— in fifty-three years I ain't never heard of one vanishing so goddamn fast!"

Frank thought it best to go along with the plan, if for no other reason than he couldn't suggest an alternative, much less a better one. They did as he instructed but the rock yielded up nothing but its inscrutable craggy face, marked with numerous yet tiny cracks which even a mouse would have had trouble crawling into. It slowly—yet still disbelievingly—became apparent to Lee Merriam and the other two that the tunnel had gone, that the rock had sealed up its secret places.

The other man called Frank said, "I don't believe this is happening to me. For chrissakes it's a dream; somebody tell me I'm dreaming."

"You're dreaming," said Lee Merriam. "Does that make you feel any better?"

"Do you reckon we'll get out?" Jerry said in a high nervous voice. He was the one, Frank recalled, who had been pleased that the chasm prevented them going any further. Now they were trapped on the ledge, with no way forward and no way back.

"Okay, take it easy," Lee Merriam said. "We've got somebody with us who knows plenty about climbing underground. Just stay calm, listen closely, and do as he says."

Frank was about to ask the name of this super-hero who was going to save them all with his marvellous skill and vast experience when he realized it was him. He thought of his eight weekend trips underground—in what had been a curbside gutter compared to this—and wondered whether he should correct Lee Merriam on a simple point of fact; he decided against it, mainly because it would have undermined his own confidence even more than theirs.

"I don't think we're gonna make it," Jerry said. He shone his lamp wildly in all directions, blinding everybody, and Lee Merriam told him to shut up, embroidering it with a couple of ripe obscenities to lend weight.

He went on, "This shaft has to lead somewhere. Maybe it cuts right through some of the old tunnels—"

"And maybe it doesn't," said the other man called Frank, who believed himself to be dreaming. "What if we just keep on going down and down and down? We're a mile underground already. For chrissakes, Lee, don't feed us bullshit."

"What do you intend to do—stand on the ledge till

207

your knees start to rot? There's a way out, I know it. There has to be." He said to Frank, "What do you think? Do we see how far the ledge goes or do we try it with the ropes?"

"How much rope have we got?"

"Eighty feet altogether."

"Let's keep to the ledge. As you say, it might intersect with a tunnel or one of the old workings. And I think we should only use two lamps and save the batteries on the other two."

Lee Merriam agreed. He switched his lamp off and told the other Frank to do the same. "Stick close to Jerry," he said. "If we all stay within touching distance we should be okay."

Frank didn't share his optimism; he was wondering what else the mountain had in store for them. If the tunnel had been deliberately sealed behind them, and this ledge conveniently provided, perhaps they were being led somewhere—or to something—they were meant to see and experience. There could be little doubt now that behind all this there was an intelligence of some kind: a conscious life-force that was planning and controlling everything that happened. Was it the mountain, or the Earth itself, or even the particles streaking in from the center of the Galaxy? And what seemed strangest of all was why something on such a scale should take an especial interest in *them*. Why had they been chosen . . . and for what purpose?

Their progress was slow and tentative. The ledge was strewn with small boulders and in places had crumbled away to a thin uneven strip less than a foot wide, so that every step had to be taken with care and due deliberation. It was hard to tell if they were keeping roughly to the same level or gradually descending—with no external point of reference their senses were confined to the ledge in front of them, the rock face to their left, and the empty black nothingness on their right.

In a curious way that surprised even him, Frank had become fatalistic about the situation in which they found themselves. He reasoned that if the mountain had gone to all the trouble of getting them this far (with presumably some ultimate objective in view) it wasn't going to leave them fumbling about in the dark forever; nor did it seem likely that the mountain was planning to dispose of them when it could have done so already, quite easily, in any number of ways.

They went on, feeling their way cautiously, using whatever handholds the rock face afforded them. Once a small boulder was dislodged and rolled over the edge out of sight; they paused and listened and waited for minutes without hearing it strike bottom.

Jerry murmured, "Jee-zuz!"

It was the last thing he heard Jerry—or any of them say.

Frank stepped forward, testing the ledge to see if it would bear his weight, and after committing himself the rock disintegrated and gave way under his foot and he fell headlong into the void. He was still clutching the lamp, as if it might save him, and by its light he saw the walls of the shaft begin to gather speed and then blur, rushing past in the spinning beam of light. It was as though he was stationary and they were moving—he felt no sensation of falling, only his body tumbling over and over in a slow-motion dream.

What at first he had taken to be the rush of air in his ears slowly resolved itself into a low moaning sound that reached him from the depths: it was the void of the mountain and the chant of the Telluric Faith rolled into one long mournful funereal drone.

CHAPTER FOUR

He was falling to the center of the Earth.

Time and space became abstractions of a greater infinity. He knew that he was inside the body of the living planet. He thought: Is this the place that Cabel calls the Ultimate Void? Will I continue to fall to the inner core of the planet where the molten rock surges like a sea of fire? And then he began to listen—because from somewhere beyond his comprehension a quiet yet insistent voice was speaking directly into his mind . . .

The human brain contains one hundred thousand million cells.

All was darkness. There was no sensation. His body was suspended in the void. He might have been inside the living Earth or outside the biosphere in the furthest reaches of space. From nowhere, it seemed, knowledge was being imparted to him, transmitted from an unknown source . . .

The Galaxy contains one hundred thousand million stars.

Had this knowledge come from the Earth, or from the Sun, or somewhere deeper in space, toward the center of the Galaxy? The voice went gently on . . .

Each star is a cell in a Hyper-Brain of galactic dimensions.

There are thousands of millions of galaxies in the Universe.

Each and every galaxy is a Hyper-Brain and together they form the Conscious Universe.

The knowledge had entered his mind without his being aware of who had placed it there, or how, or why. He simply knew. How could he have acquired such knowledge? And why had he been chosen to receive it?

More secrets awaited him.

The cells in the human brain conduct electrochemical impulses

The stars in the Hyper-Brain conduct particles of pure energy.

Electrochemical impulses are the communicating links which constitute thought, reasoning, memory, and conscious self-awareness in the human organism.

Particles of pure energy are the communicating links which constitute thought, reasoning, memory, and conscious self-awareness in the galactic organism.

Was this, then, the function of neutrinos—to transmit messages at the speed of light from star-cell to star-cell? Did they form the neurological pathways of the galactic Hyper-Brain? Stellar fusion emitted neutrinos just as brain cells transmitted electrochemical impulses. The pattern was maintained from the human level to the cosmic. The Galaxy was a brain and the Sun a single nerve cell amongst one hundred thousand million.

As below, so above.

The human brain perceives the Hyper-Brain.

The Hyper-Brain perceives the Conscious Universe.

Now he could see clearly the Galaxy moving through time and space. It was a conscious being which knows itself to be an individual life form in the Universe. There were thousands of millions of other galaxies, each one possessing intelligence, each one aware of itself as an individual consciousness.

They were able to communicate. Just as the human brain had the ability to exchange thoughts and ideas, so it was possible for Hyper-Brain to converse with Hyper-Brain: the Universe was filled with the whispering of a thousand million conscious beings. And the Universe itself was the supreme conscious being for which there was only—could only be—One Name.

But the mystery of how he knew these things amazed him; he seemed to have become aware of them instinctively, as if the knowledge had materialized out of nowhere and unfolded within his mind.

But there were still questions. If neutrinos formed the neurological pathways between star-cells, what function did antineutrinos have? Was it part of the overall design that they should decay into *antitrimuons,* producing vast quantities of lethal radiation? What would be the equivalent in the human brain? Possibly a condition similar to a sudden discharge of electrical energy leading to a brainstorm—

A galactic brainstorm?

Was this what had awakened the Earth from primordial slumber? Were antineutrinos a type of renegade particle which were the cause on the galactic level of something resembling a brain seizure? In human beings such a condition would give rise to convulsions and brief surges of violence and uncontrollable rage. And wasn't this precisely what had been happening to the Earth?

He recalled that it was possible to artifically stimulate the brain with electrodes placed at certain points so as to produce the effect of a seizure. How could this be achieved on the galactic level? How else but by building up a concentrated source of radiation which would then trigger the *antitrimuon* events to produce a sudden discharge of radioactive energy—leading to brain seizure. This source of radiation, as he now knew, was in the detection chamber: the tanks contained an accumulation of argon-37 which when released would trigger the *antitrimuon* events. An electrode had been placed deep in the Hyper-Brain and one brief sharp shock to the cerebrum would be the signal for a violent seizure—clusters of star-cells discharging energy to produce a galactic brainstorm.

It was as though the Earth was an infinitesimally small yet malignant nerve cell in the Hyper-Brain of the Galaxy. It was at the point of the electrode, waiting for the signal to erupt into life. And when it did—when the detection tanks released the radioactive trigger—what then?

His mind reached out in the blackness, seeking the answer.

And the answer came, delivered in a voice that was vibrant and charged with feeling, saying:

"For too long they have ignored the warning of the Ultimate Void. And now the Earth speaks for us . . . now is come the day of reckoning when the floodwaters will rise up and the breath of life will be taken from them and they will be destroyed from the living Earth for evermore!"

It was a voice he remembered—the voice of Cabel —issuing from the mouth of Professor Edmund Friedmann.

The gantry had become his pulpit. He stood with arms extended, tall and spare in the one-piece black suit, his face hidden in the shadow cast by the wide brim of his hat. His voice was high and tremulous as he preached to the assembled congregation: the four stainless steel detection tanks which gleamed like huge silver tombs in the harsh glare of the overhead arc-lights.

Leach had said that Professor Friedmann had come below to prepare the way. Did Friedmann believe he had a mission to make straight the path for the cosmic intelligence reaching the Earth from the center of the Galaxy? He had known all along that the antineutrinos were a form of galactic communication, but what he hadn't realized was the effect they would have on the geophysical structure of the Earth —and the radiation that would result from antineu-trino-*antitrimuon* interaction.

Professor Friedmann was unaware that in addition to the detection tanks he had a human congregation of one. His gaze was not outwardly-directed but focused on the inner secrets which the cosmos had yielded up to him. They swam before his eyes like the exploding birth of stars, like the busy humming world of nuclear particles. Nothing on the human scale had relevance; only the mysteries of the Omniverse and the Ultimate Void, the Greater and Lesser Bodies extending above and below, the twelve sacred levels which constituted the religious doctrine of the Telluric Faith.

Frank Kersh also had a mission to fulfil. Twice now the mountain had come to his aid and brought him to the detection chamber—yet he still didn't understand what was expected of him. Another intelligence (the Hyper-Brain?) had communicated something of the underlying truth; it had made manifest its intensions by bringing him here, but for what purpose?

He slowly began to ascend the metal stairway, keeping his eyes on the tall straight figure in black. Professor Friedmann was intent on his sermon, oblivious to anything that might be taking place in the real physical world; his voice had acquired the peculiarly hypnotic fervor that Frank remembered from the torchlight gathering in the square.

It was now clear how Cabel had been able to predict the severe climatic changes: his prophesy had been based on the scientific data obtained by the Project. The high incidence of antineutrino detection had pointed to a disruption of the biosphere, which Friedmann had reinterpreted in religious terms for the benefit of his followers. And when the freak thunderstorms and violent tremors swept along the Roaring Fork Valley they had proved conclusively the extent of his predictive powers and the truth of what he preached.

His message was Destruction—and the elements had

dutifully played their part in bringing it about.

"And now the time is come when the forces within the living Earth shall be awakened. They have slept throughout all the ages of mankind, since that first instant when their conscious being was transformed from whirling gas into the body of this planet. They have waited patiently for release, these elemental forces of nature, for the moment when the message from beyond would arouse them from their slumber—"

He suddenly raised the black rods of his arms high above his head, fingers splayed like pale stars.

"Within these holy vessels resides the power of the Cosmic World! It has come to us from the infinite depths of space, from the center of our Galaxy. This power shall descend to the Ultimate Void within the body of the sleeping Earth. The waters shall rise up and the rocks shall be split asunder and the heavens shall clash as they receive the breath of life. Man will be destroyed from the face of the Earth—both man, and beast, and the creeping thing, and the fowls of the air. Behold I, even I, do bring a flood of waters upon the Earth, to destroy all flesh, and everything that is in the Earth shall die!"

It was evident that Professor Friedmann believed himself to be invested with divine power: he was the human instrument of the consciousness which permeated the Galaxy. Through his ministry the Earth would reawaken.

Frank stepped onto the gantry. Below him the tanks seemed to rise from the floor of the chamber like monstrous rectangular icebergs. There was no outward sign of the activity within them as the radioactive atoms of argon-37 built up to the level when they would become unstable—and what happened thereafter would be ample confirmation of Professor Friedmann's prophesy of cataclysmic destruction.

He glanced toward the row of consoles which housed the recording equipment and was surprised to see that it was still working. The needles hovered in the dials, registering the particle interactions, and a moving ribbon of graph-paper charted the rise in nuclear activity. How soon before the condition inside the detection tanks reached optimum? Was the process even at this moment too far advanced to bring into operation the usual fail-safe procedure?

Professor Friedmann paused in his oratory and turned abruptly. Without the blue-tinted spectacles his eyes seemed naked, almost vulnerable, a vague myopic dullness about them like those of a man lost in a fog.

"Karl . . . ?"

"No, is isn't Karl. Frank Kersh."

The name meant nothing. Friedmann moved away from the rail, holding his head to one side, inquisitively, like an old man straining to hear. There was something disjointed about his stance. He said:

"We have received the message from the Cosmic World. It has come from the galactic center, passed through the twelve levels of Telluric consciousness, and is about to enter the Ultimate Void."

"You've actually heard the message?" Frank said carefully.

"Oh yes." Professor Friedmann pointed to the tanks. "The message is there. Can't you hear it?" He smiled rapturously. "The Earth hears and will soon awaken. Listen!"

From deep within the core, as if obeying him, a shock-wave reverberated through thousands of miles of iron-magnesium mantle to the granitic crust. It grew in intensity, like a gathering roll of thunder, and the chamber trembled. Frank felt the gantry shift under his feet. He thought: Either that was a damn lucky guess or he really does have control over the Ultimate Void—wherever and whatever that is.

Frank edged slowly toward the row of consoles. It was essential that he check the level of interaction in the tanks.

Friedmann said, "Are you a member of the Faith? Do you believe in Earth Power?"

Frank nodded, wondering just how much sanity Professor Friedmann retained. Had he been affected by the radiation to the same degree as the four men who had died, so that even now the tumor was eating away at the soft tissue of his brain? Leach had slipped over the edge into babbling lunacy and it might be that Friedmann wouldn't be too long in following him.

"I have prepared the way," Friedmann said. He took a step forward. He looked at Frank as if he were gazing into the distance. "Do you realize that after five billion years the Earth is about to regain its consciousness? It was formed from plasma from out of the living Sun and became the Tellus, the sentient planet. And all this time it has awaited the signal from the Cosmic World . . . the signal to reawaken!"

He moved a further step forward, partly blocking the way to the measuring equipment. Was this deliberate—did he know very well who Frank was and what he was trying to do—or was he genuinely lost in visions, his head filled with the plasma of madness?

Frank said, "But if your prophesy comes true, won't the members of the Faith also lose their lives? If the mountain splits open and the waters rise up, then surely everyone will perish. Isn't this so?"

"Everyone will perish," Friedmann agreed, almost dreamily. He seemed to relish the notion. "Everyone except the Tellurians."

"You mean the members of the Faith?"

"No, no. You do not understand. The Tellurians awaiting the signal."

He meant the babies. The babies were the Tellurians.

Friedmann went on, his voice quite gentle now:

"They have been endowed with the intelligence of the Cosmic World. They are to become the true inhabitants of the planet Earth. From them will spring a new species of human being that will live in harmony with Tellus."

It seemed that Professor Friedmann, even in his madness (or perhaps because of it) had perceived the significance and purpose of the galactic intelligence which had directed the stream of antineutrinos toward the Earth. There was to be an awakening not only of the planet but also of a species which would inherit the Earth.

From deep underground another tremor shook the chamber and the gantry creaked, like the sound of metal in pain. Frank looked past Friedmann's shoulder to the recording consoles and saw the needles swinging wildly, registering the high rate of particle interaction. He knew it was too late: the concentration of argon-37 in the tanks had reached the critical level. There was nothing anyone could to to prevent a massive leakage of radiation that would act as a device to trigger the *antitrimuon* events—which would in turn contaminate the interior of the mountain and everything trapped there.

Freidmann came a sudden step nearer. His manner was intimidating. As if reading Frank's mind he said:

"You can do nothing to alter the destiny of the Cosmic World. Very soon the signal will be released and the Tellurians will become the true and rightful inhabitants of Tellus. The time of awakening is with us at last . . . "

His head was bent to one side, as if he were listening for the signal, and the light fell on his neck. There was something there, attached to him, and it took Frank a moment to realize that it was a growth of some kind, a scaly eruption of scabious tissue. Friedmann was physically decomposing, giving off the evil smell that permeated the entire mountain. He was decaying as the needles of radiation penetrated his flesh and infected the cells with a creeping malignant tumor.

And Frank thought: It must be happening to me, too. The radiation from the tanks is filling the chamber, an invisible yet deadly stream of particles infiltrating brain and body and infecting them with a cancerous growth.

There was the feverish light of pure madness in Friedmann's eyes. He raised his arms high in a gesture that was half worship, half supplication, and Frank saw that his hands were flaking away to reveal the raw musculature and skeletal structure beneath. His skin had the dead white powdery texture of chalk.

"The way is open, the path has been made straight,

life forms, the basis for being throughout the entire Universe.

By a random interaction of particles (pure chance? an accident?) something that called itself Frank Kersh had been brought into existence. He might have been any one of a billion people, or not a person at all, the molecules that made up his body scattered far and wide at the ends of time and space. The physical machine which housed him was a temporary accommodation, of no real significance, lasting less than a fraction of a nano-second on the cosmic time-scale. The machine would eventually decay and die and the atoms would assume some other form; the part of him that constituted his conscious awareness would be transferred to something else—he would continue to live, to physically exist, in the greater body that some called the Conscious Universe, and others called God.

Looking down the slope of his body he saw a small group of people climbing toward him, seeking the higher ground above the encroaching floodwater. One of them was a young girl with red hair, and another a short fat middle-aged man who was laboring with difficulty, pausing every few steps to grunt and wheeze and catch his breath. They were still a long way below him and perhaps wouldn't need to climb up to this height, which he hoped was the case, because he was perfectly happy to remain undisturbed, high above everything else, gazing out across the placid pond which separated him from his neighbors.

the Earth awaits you! Cabel hears and obeys the message from the Cosmic World—let the water rise up and the mountain split asunder and let Tellus return to its former consciousness and the full glory of cosmic life!"

The mountain, it seemed, had heard his exhortation, and was about to heed it, for a fierce shock ripped through the sub-strata and the floor of the chamber split open in a series of jagged diagonal cracks. The concrete foundations on which the gantry rested crumbled away to dust and the entire steel edifice tilted and heeled over toward the tanks so that they were both thrown against the rail, like passengers clinging to the stern of a sinking ship.

The tanks too had been disturbed, their stainless steel sides creaking and buckling as the floor of the chamber shifted, and with the sound of a screeching live thing caught in a trap the metal was torn apart and 600,000 gallons of radioactive perchloroethylene poured from the shattered tanks and rose up in a green tide.

Frank held on to the rail as the foaming flood raced toward the leaning gantry, bracing himself for the shock of impact, and from the corner of his eye saw Professor Friedmann's mad staring face infused with an expression of joyous exhultation, almost one of rapture as if in anticipation of the moment of fulfillment.

The structure tilted even more as the wave hit and rushed between the struts so that the two of them were suspended above the swirling green fluid, looking down on it with only the metal rail to cling to, separating them by no more than a couple of feet.

But Friedmann—even had he wanted to—couldn't hold on: his hands had atrophied to raw peeling flesh and crude bone claws which were no longer able to maintain their grip, and he slithered between the rail and the angled floor of the gantry. In less than a second he was gone, his black one-piece overall ballooning in the manner of a comic cartoon figure, his grey razored head soon lost in the swirl of green fluid which lapped at the supports. The last image Frank had of him was a skeletal hand clutching uselessly at nothing before it was sucked under; there was a final eddying slurp as the perchloroethylene claimed its first victim, the self-proclaimed prophet of the Telluric Faith.

He's fulfilled his mission, Frank thought, and brought about the awakening of the planet. Either by design or accident he's unleashed the radiation which will trigger the antineutrino-*antitrimuon* interaction —like placing the electrode in the vital spot in the human brain and generating enough electrical energy to stimulate a violent seizure.

He looked at his own hands gripping the rail, expecting to see them deteriorating from the radiation which must now be filling the chamber—penetrating everything with needles of pure energy—and was amazed that they were still recognizably his own, apparently suffering no adverse effect. This couldn't be: it was plainly impossible: it was like being inside the core of the atomic reactor, the level of radiation so high that living tissue couldn't withstand for more than a few minutes this sustained attack on its cellular structure. Yet he was still (he thought he was) thinking rationally, aware of his surroundings, knowing that Professor Friedmann was dead and he remained alive and in possession of his faculties.

There was only one possible explanation—an intelligence beyond his comprehension was exerting a greater force to counteract the intense storm of radioactivity caused by the release of argon-37.

And it could only be the same intelligence that had communicated to him during this mysterious "fall" toward the inner void, when the voice had entered his mind and spoken of the secrets of the Galaxy: a conscious being amongst thousands of millions of others in the Universe.

The perchloroethylene was draining from the chamber, its green frothing surface sinking way from him as it poured deeper into the Earth through the fissures which had been opened up by the tremor. Gradually the shattered tanks were revealed and the buckled leaning structure of the gantry, poised at a precarious angle as if defying the law of gravity. The recording equipment lay in a mangled heap, wedged against the rail, its weight threatened to overbalance the spindly framework of twisted girders.

Moving slowly from strut to strut, Frank descended to the floor of the chamber, now covered with a sticky green substance that reminded him of the moldering decay on the barks of trees. There was no sign of Professor Friedmann's body, which must have been swept underground and was by now several miles deep within the mantle of the Earth. The cracks which had split the chamber were too wide to cross; the only way out, as far as he knew, was through the main tunnel which led to the shaft, but he couldn't get to it; after all this was he to be trapped in the depths of the mine amidst the wreckage of the solar neutrino research experiment? It seemed the ultimate point of futility that so much had happened, so much had been revealed, and yet everything had finally conspired to place him in his seemingly impossible situation.

The mountain began to shake. It was like a huge prehistoric beast coming alive after millions of years, a slow grinding awakening as one by one its senses became alerted. He felt it move, and again he experienced the feeling that he was inside the body of a living animal, a tiny parasite in the stomach sac of something too huge to notice it.

He thought: Supposing Friedmann was right? What if the Earth had coalesced out of "conscious" plasma and was now, five billion years later, regaining its awareness? But he didn't know what to think any more. The rationality of his thought processes, in which he had taken so much pride and smug satisfaction, was no longer able to cope with the sequence of bizarre circumstances, the apparent irrationality of the Telluric gospel, the existence of vibrating mirror-like black rocks . . .

He had forgotten the black rock. It was sealing the main tunnel, shutting off the detection chamber from the outside world. Or had it fulfilled its purpose in allowing Friedmann to prepare the way? Now that the mountain was alive had it returned once more to the inner depths, the Ultimate Void?

The ground lurched beneath him and he was jerked off his feet and sent sprawling in ·the odious green slime. The jagged gaping cracks were widening, crumbling away at the edges, the entire floor of the chamber patterned with them like a pool of splintered green ice. He was marooned on a diamond-shaped piece of rock whose surface was smooth and slimy, providing no purchase for his slithering arms and legs. It seemed that the mountain had saved him twice in order that he might witness its final cataclysmic triumph—and now it was done with him and he was to follow Friedmann as the next sacrificial victim.

Above him the roof of the chamber began to disintegrate. The arc lights swung crazily, like revolving searchlights, flickered and went out. He was in complete and utter darkness, spread eagled on a splinter of rock, feeling the vibrations of the Earth in every part of his body as if he were joined to it; his body and the living Earth were as one, the same substance, the same flesh, the same rock.

And he knew that this was so. The molecules and atoms and subnuclear particles throughout all creation were made up of the self-same constituent parts. The matter in the stars was identical to the matter in his own body—the ingredients for life had been formed within stars, so he himself and every other living creature was a product of star-stuff. I came from the stars, he told himself, experiencing a strange, and almost a wondrous, excitement. The stars live through me, they find their living form and consciousness through my being. We are all the same throughout the Universe: all matter and energy emanating from the same source. The Sun and the Earth and my body are all living entities in the sight of the Conscious Universe.

He felt like weeping. The rock shook against him like a release of emotion. There was a strange sense of relief as if it didn't matter any more how or in what form his consciousness found expression. Why should it make any difference when everything was of the one indivisible substance, each after its own fashion alive and equally sacred? And just as the stars lived through him, he would live through the Earth, become part of its sentient being.

They were all one: as above, so below.

The calm he now felt seemed infinite. The blackness all around soothed him, and he thought: When Friedmann spoke of the Ultimate Void he was referring to the still small center which exists inside every living thing. Every creature. Every plant. Every stone. There is a secret inner place which even science can't penetrate, no matter how deeply it probes into the subnuclear world. An area of stillness at the center of all things.

He lay on the rock. It was very quiet. Looking upward he saw a shape picked out in pinpricks of light: the seven stars forming The Plough, their pointers marking the position of the Pole Star. And further beyond the great spangled W of Cassiopeia, situated in the Milky Way.

Then the sky was ablaze with stars, from horizon to horizon, more than he could recall ever having seen before. They were spread across the dark heavens like a million eyes looking down on him, even as he watched them; and when a faint chill breeze touched his face he knew that he was gazing into the Universe from the Mount of the Holy Cross.

CHAPTER SIX

The fierce tremors had ravaged the townships along the Roaring Fork Valley from as far east as Malta through Eagel to Rifle in the west—and worse, had opened up the fault line which ran parallel with Eagle River and underneath the Great Eagle Dam. But so far the Dam had held. During the night the tremors continued, inching apart the two mountain ranges, topped by the Mount of the Holy Cross on one side of the Valley and Mount Powell on the other.

Radium had been unaffected, though the tremors had been felt with sufficient vigór for many of the townspeople to pitch tents in the fields and spend the night wrapped up in sleeping bags.

It was cold on the granite heights of the mountain but even so Frank waited for the dawn with a kind of stoic forbearance that amounted almost to fatalism. It seemed that he was alone on the top of the world, with the vivid stars near enough to touch, and below him the dark Earth shaken and trembling by the forces at work in the inner core of the planet.

The starlight was brilliant, coating the rising granite peak with a soft silvery sheen. He thought how that light had travelled for thousands of years to bathe the mountain in its radiance; it had begun its journey when the Universe was young, before the Earth had been born, and had survived those countless light years with the sole purpose of expending itself here on the mountain. He wondered if the light from the stars knew this, knew of the purpose planned for it so long ago, and decided that light was selfless and therefore wouldn't care what it was used to illuminate. But he was glad to be there to perceive the beauty of the light bathing the mountain; somehow it made the journey seem worthwhile that a sentient creature had seen and appreciated the starlight's effect on this speck of matter circling in the void. His senses told him it was beautiful, and this was reason enough.

He was on the eastern slope and so the Sun's first rays struck like lances across the Valley from the distant peaks of the Rocky Mountain range, directly into his eyes. They lit up the severe granite face of the mountain, and then further below the golden banks of aspens which descended into the shadowed pool of the Valley itself.

Below him he could see the bright orange tracery of the winding gear, etched like a hierograph against the dull red circle of the compound with its cluster of huts, and as the light intensified he could even make out dark specks of figures moving to and fro.

Helen and her father were probably amongst them, waiting for news of the rescue teams . . . and this made him wonder what had happened to Lee Merriam and the two men trapped on the ledge. They would assume he was dead, and if they ever made it back to the surface that was the story they would tell. And by rights he should have been dead, if not from the fall, then from the radiation released into the chamber by the argon-37. Friedmann had been affected by it, corroding away to nothing, but he had escaped physical harm. The knowledge of this he found discomforting; it was almost as if he knew himself to be morally responsible for a crime and by some mysterious quirk of circumstance had been let off; retribution suspended.

From far off in the distance a noise came to his ears. It was the sound of someone tearing huge sheets of cardboard, very slowly and methodically, with great patience. His eye was attracted by a pale glimmer along the Valley and he knew even before his senses had registered the fact that the fault had crept inexorably wider and the waters of the Dam had burst through the concrete barrier and were now rushing in a white fury toward the townships along the Eagle River.

It was what he had been waiting for.

The rolling wall of water gathered force and speed, and, hemmed in by the two mountain ranges standing shoulder to shoulder, swept along the Roaring Fork Valley in a smooth imperturbable flow that swallowed up one by one Red Cliff, Mintburn, Avon, Eagle, Gypsum, Dotsero, New Castle, Silt, Rifle and De Beque. It was accomplished with such ease, and from this distance, high on the mountain, lacking all sound and fury, that he wondered if it was a vision of things to come, a silent dream that foretold a disaster that had yet to happen.

But the reality lay before him, just as Cabel had prophesied. In place of the Valley there was now a

231

long narrow body of water upon whose turbulant surface the fractured reflection of Mount Powell glittered and broke in a thousand fragments. Beyond the mountain, safe and untouched by the waters, the town of Radium, and the hospital, and . . . the Tellurians?

The cold had penetrated right through him but he didn't seem to mind. Physical sensation had left him and he was quite content to look down on the shimmering flatness of water which lay before the Mount of the Holy Cross; this was his resting place, a high vantage point from which he could observe what had become a tranquil scene of sky, mountains, and water, with no human habitation in sight. It seemed he would be happy to remain here forever, a passive observer of this natural landscape: unspoiled, silent except for the wind, returned to the condition as it must have been before man trod upon the Earth.

Strangely, the fact that people had perished down there in the Valley didn't stir in him the pity or anguish that he might have expected. It wasn't that he regarded their lives as worthless, but rather that he now firmly believed that nothing could ever die. Just as matter was indestructible, assuming another form or being transferred into energy, so he was convinced that life couldn't be destroyed but was simply transmuted into another form of life, the atoms of a human being merging once more into the great body of the Earth from whence they had sprung.

Everything contained life in one sense or another and it made no difference if you lived as a warm-blooded creature, as a plant, or a rock, or as whirling gas in space. Matter and energy were the only true

CHAPTER SEVEN

They came to a gentler part of the slope where it was possible to stand almost upright without overbalancing. There was a thin patch of harsh dark green grass, sprinkled with a few pale flowers, adhering tenaciously to the grey shale, and in the clear horizontal sunlight it was like a little oasis of warmth and comfort on the bleak mountainside.

Cal Renfield said, "This is for me. I stop right here." He stood for a moment holding his stomach with both hands and then lowered himself to a reclining position. His chest heaved with the effort of climbing and the effect of the more rarified air at this higher altitude.

One of the other men said, "I guess we're safe enough here. The level is static, seems to me. Wouldn't you say so?" he appealed to the others.

Nobody took the trouble to reply, but for an answer flopped down on the grass, taking in deep lungfuls of air; their mood was somber and withdrawn, their stamina exhausted as much by the long night's vigil as by the exertions of the climb.

The group was what remained of the personnel on

on the Deep Hole Project: six technical staff and two maintenance engineers. The mine had claimed five more victims in the past twelve hours, including the Project leader, and that numbing fact along with the severe tremors and the breaching of the Great Eagle Dam had drained them of everything but the most dazed noncommittal response. There was simply nothing to say that would alter what had happened or make sense of it: they had to accept and come to terms with it each in their own way.

Helen found it impossible to accept. Even now she hadn't given up hoping, and for only the second time in her adult life had prayed to an invisible being, offered up a silent but heartfelt prayer to something in which she didn't believe in a last desperate plea that a miracle would happen and the four men who had gone looking for Professor Friedmann would suddenly magically appear from the mine shaft, faces streaked with dust, eyes red-raw, but safe and sound, alive and breathing, not maimed or injured or harmed in any way. She still believed it to be possible, even though the engineer who had led the back-up team had insisted that any hope there might have been had long since faded.

"Any chance they had disappeared the second the Dam broke," he told her. "That's if the radiation didn't get them first."

"But the level of the water didn't reach the head of the mine," Helen said, distraught.

The engineer shook his head. "It doesn't have to. The tunnel they were in is nearly a mile underground, and with that volume of water in the Valley there must be a hundred access points leading to the lower level. "I'm sorry, but there it is—the Telluride Mine is flooded right up to the brim. Anyone in there is not only underground but underwater as well."

Now she looked down on the bright orange steelwork above the mine-head, the helplessness so strong inside her that she felt physically sick. What if a miracle had occurred and they had managed to find a pocket of air, enough to keep them alive until a rescue team got to them? It was still possible, wasn't it? Why couldn't these people do something instead of sitting here on the side of the mountain in the clear morning sunlight? They were alive, breathing fresh air, while underground there could be four men clinging to the last vestiges of life, counting every breath and praying it wasn't to be their last.

Helen turned her head away from the flooded Valley and looked up toward the gaunt granite peak of the mountain with its light powdering of snow. For once it was free of cloud, standing sharp and black and slab-like against the pale washed blue of the sky. It reminded her of a monolith, a monument of some kind, though she couldn't think what event or person it had been erected to commemorate.